CW00540139

About the Author

Born and raised in West Yorkshire, aye up, I left school at sixteen and went to beauty college to become a make-up artist (in truth, I just hoped to get a ticket to Hollywood so I could marry Brad Pitt). Since that didn't work, after dabbling in some modelling, I worked as a legal secretary, sat some exams and, eight years later, qualified as a solicitor. I met the man of my dreams, (I knew he was Mr Right as he made my bowels move). We have been married for fifteen years, live near York and have two amazing children.

Ah, Feck it

Nicki Todd

Ah, Feck it

Cover Illustration by Cathy Evangelista

Olympia Publishers
London

www.olympiapublishers.com
OLYMPIA PAPERBACK EDITION

A CIP catalogue record for this title is
available from the British Library.

ISBN: 978-1-84897-830-0

This is a work of fiction.
Names, characters, places and incidents originate from the writer's
imagination. Any resemblance to actual persons, living or dead, is
purely coincidental.

First Published in 2017

Olympia Publishers
60 Cannon Street
London
EC4N 6NP

Printed in Great Britain

Dedication

For Hubby, who is my rock, and blessed with the patience of a saint.

Acknowledgments

First and foremost, to my family.

To Hubby, who has sat patiently and listened to the audio version of my book as it has progressed.

To my daughter, who has learnt to make her own tea so "Mummy can write."

To my son, thanks for being such a good baby allowing me the time to write this book.

To my mum, my number one fan. It is from you I have this twisted sense of humour.

To the friends who have supported me unquestionably. Not only have they laughed at my jokes, but kept me going, offering encouragement and support.

I would like to say a huge thank you to my friend, Emma Garcia, author of *Never Google Heartbreak*, who encouraged me to start writing.

I would like also like to thank all the staff at Olympia Publishing House for signing me up. As a new writer, it isn't easy getting your work out there. Thank you for investing your time into my book.

Chapter One
School

So I've done the romance bit, met the man of my dreams, lah, dee, dah. I had the castle type wedding (I got bored and went to bed at 11.30, every other bugger drank the free fizz). I got pregnant, I'm in baby bliss heaven. The world will now be perfect... as we know, is it heck, disaster strikes. A tsunami hits our lives, and the reason this one is worse is that there's no one to pull the plug. I mean, this thing is with you 24/7, no weekend off, no bank holidays. It's an endless struggle, a thankless task. Parenthood is not what they say it is. Before you had a baby you'd never even heard of colic? If someone had said it to me, I'd have thought it was a local rock band. Why don't they put warnings on those leaflets and books when you are trying for a baby? Warning: Your baby may develop colic. There is no cure, the doctors won't believe you, and you will purchase every possible brand of medication on display in Boots, including purchasing anti-colic bottles. You will engage in baby massage and take your baby to a chiropractor. In those first twelve weeks, you will blow the entire savings you had for your maternity leave. It's pure torture.

I play the perfect mother card: outwardly, life is rosy, fulfilled, my matching nappy bag and pram are the symbol of perfect motherhood. 'I have succeeded in life, I have borne a child and I have a matching set to prove it.' Deep down, I just want to drink gin and eat cake! But you get over it, they grow up, the little darlings develop a personality. One minute I want to actually strangle her (I know social services will probably want to remove my child for saying that, but I never did so there's no due cause), and the next, I feel like my heart will pop out my chest and wrap itself around this gorgeous creature I created. Nurturing to narcotics – who knew!

Anyway, the point of this story is not the 'meeting the only man I will ever shag for the REST of my life and playing happy families' but it's the 'Ever After' part. The part where my five-year-old tells me to 'fuck off' in the playground, right in front of the toffee-nosed cake-making bitches whose kids only know how to say 'organic' and 'evolutionary mummy'. Tossers!

So, you want to know where this story starts. Well, it starts right in the playground, walking said five-year-old daughter to her school (her name is actually Davina, don't suppose it's appropriate to call her 'said five-year-old'!). She's nervous, I'm more nervous – will she bite anyone today? Is it acceptable to have Weetabix in my hair and put this coloured shirt with these coloured trousers? Clearly not, for once I hit that expanse of space, I soon realise where the battle lines are drawn. Suddenly, despite a great effort to not be a 'chav', I actually find myself stood with the other chavs! Mother nature and her crew are stood at the far side of the playground and the force field that surrounds them is unbreakable. I will not penetrate this, particularly in this outfit and especially since my child has just displayed her pants. Oh crap. Maybe I misjudged the chavs? Maybe there is a class in there that are like me? Or maybe not. "Get here, you fuckin little shite." Ah, okay. I slide slightly towards the bit in the middle, between the chavs and mother heaven and then I realise, there are a couple more people like me in this group. The so-called 'outsiders, misfits'; give them a name, any name, they'll just be glad of the attention. So I join the middle circle and soon realise their children are like mine. When the gay guy's son runs up to me and asks if I have a 'vagina', I realise this actually might be a group I fit into.

The conversation is light. I really can only make small talk because my eyes are forever watching that little devil darling that belongs to me, but I manage a few hellos. Then, with a deafening blow, that bell rings and it takes me straight back to being five years old and prized away from my mother's arm. Oh, how it hurt – the pain. They grabbed your arm and took you in and that was it for the next eleven years, bloody torture. I look around for my poor, undeserving child, but realise she's already gone inside. Darn, the teachers these days, they just don't have the fear factor.

Shuffling feet, I walk out the school gates. Forlorn, like I've just lost a limb. My poor baby, poor me, my baby, my poor baby... but, hang on... they've taken her, until 3.35 p.m. Hang on, that's like a whole (fingers required) six hours and forty-five minutes! Jesus wept. I'm child free, I'm solo. The giddiness is a like a

Jagerbomb shot five times over. I find myself running back to the car, yes, running, I haven't done that in seven years (two years of trying and being saintly towards my body, no exercise, no bad food, just sex, sex and more sex).

I reach home and open the door. The sound of nothingness is upon me. Ohhh, how I love that sound. Ohhh, how I've wanted to hear that sound for the past five years. I don't quite know what to do, so it seems sensible to do something solitary. I boil the kettle, pour myself a coffee, put on *This Morning* and grab the pile of *25 Beautiful Homes* magazines I've been collecting since 2010. This is good. I'm looking, but suddenly I realise I no longer actually give a shit what my house looks like. What has happened? Gone are the days of filter coffee, a settee and *25 Beautiful Homes* magazine. It doesn't matter anymore, but why? Why doesn't it matter? This used to replicate a perfect Sunday morning. I walk past the mirror and catch a glimpse of myself. Who is this person? I look like a cross between Nanny McPhee (the ugly version) and Jabba the Hutt. What happened to me? I cannot think about it. I pick up the remote and realise I am drawn to CBeebies, it's time for *Mr Bloom*. This is the time of day when I normally sit down with Davina and we actually watch television together. It's bonding. Actually, it's normally me insisting that she watch it because it's educational when, in reality, she just wants to crayon on my Feather and Black cushions. That same feeling reappears when I watch *Mr Bloom*. A tingle, a little sheepish – oh, but this time there is no child. Christ, where's my dildo? I think I last saw it at the back of the sock draw, covered with tights I cannot fit into. I find myself praying, *Please let us have double As*. Pete's OCD supply of batteries is now something I am actually grateful for. I dust it down, remove the fluff it collected from the back of the draw and rinse it under the tap with Palmolive soap.

The rest I need not describe, but when I emerge from my duvet, it's like 'Hey, man, I just rode a mighty fuckin' wave.' So the swagger is on now, I'd smoke but I haven't got any fags left (I smoked the last packet in the third trimester but I'll never admit it). So I waltz about the house. It's Beyoncé time. I feel like pouring myself a glass of wine to celebrate this new release of life. I truly appreciate every moment. This cannot be repeated, you can't read about this in *Woman's Own*, this is happening now and I bloody well deserve it.

So I've shaked my bootie for a while, the hours have passed without me realising. I check the clock. *Shit*. She will be back soon. *Tea*. I need to make some tea. Something healthy and nutritional; fish fingers, chips and peas will do.

After I've finished checking my still rosy cheeks in the mirror, I realise its 3.30 p.m. Bollocks. Pick up is at 3.35 p.m. It's okay, we only live three minutes from the school. I get in the car and drive to the school, but holy shit, what's happened? OMG!!! Something terrible must have happened, as cars surround the school. There is nowhere to park. My poor baby is stuck in some horrific accident in school and I cannot get to her. I abandon the car outside the 'No Parking – Disabled Person only' parking space. I race to the gates, out of breath for the one hundred yards I've just moved, and there I find all the other parents in a queue. A queue for what? To identify the bodies? Oh, shit, and there I was, masturbating to *Mr Bloom*. I realise the pace is moving slowly, there is no panic, people are chatting, even the gay guy is talking to someone casually. Oh! The crowd shuffle forwards, I am drawn in. I take a deep breath. I am still not sure what to expect at the other end: will she be laid flat out in the playground, bleeding from the head? I carry on with the mob, I push forwards until I realise the crowd is simply waiting for the gate to open. Of course, the gate, the playground gate, that's why we are queuing. I am relieved. I quietly praise myself for picking this school. Security was top of my list (after longingly searching for schools that keep children until seven p.m.) I'm through, there's no disaster – phew, thank the Lord, she's safe. My strides are slightly larger into the playground. *Yep, all is good*, our children are safe and they are coming home. Deep sigh.

Okay, I need to calm myself. I've had an afternoon off, but that's not my life anymore. My life is now filled with the joy and loving sound of my five-year-old daughter. The truth is, I'm not quite sure what to expect when the doors open. Will she come out excited to see me, or will she be crying because she doesn't want to come home? As I ponder her arrival, the gay guy walks over to me.

"I'm so worried, Lionel can be a right little shit, I just hope he's behaved."

It occurs to me that 'Lionel' is probably adopted. I am filled with admiration. To give up your life for a child who has no family to care for him is a truly selfless act. A true hero. It's much better than how I acquired my child. I just laid back, mentally wrote my shopping list, stuck my legs in the air for a good half hour after and, kapow, job done.

"Don't worry. I'm sure they've had a great day," I say. We both smile at one another, knowing there is no truth in this statement. And then it happens, the teacher appears and, like laying out the lambs to slaughter, she produces her crop. Out comes every other bugger's child except mine. Where's is she? Was I wrong, was there actually a disaster? Oh no, I see, she has been held back with Lionel. Lionel has a black eye. Davina has something that looks like blood dripping from her mouth. Crap! And there it is, the finger. Mrs Crecher points and wiggles her finger at me, symbolling for me to come over. Not me, surely not me, you mean the gay guy? Then come the two fingers and I realise it's me and the gay guy. At this point, I feel like I need a friend.

"I'm Jess by the way."

"I'm Carlton."

We both walk, almost doing the wedding march, to Mrs Crecher. It's unknown territory but somehow I know it, I've done this walk before and it never ends well. "A word, please," says Mrs Crecher. We are taken into the infants' cloakroom. I try to look at ease.

"Sit," she barks. It's at this point I see the teeth marks around her ankle, covered with some fresh blood. I sit straight away but realise too late that where you normally expect a seat to be, there's a massive drop, and my arse lands on a cold wooden bench, with my knees hitting my ears. "I was very disturbed to find Davina laid across Lionel, poking one set of fingers in his eyes and the other on his trousers." There are no words. "I was even more disturbed to hear Lionel say, 'Do it like you mean it, bitch.' I don't know what you are teaching these children but it is not acceptable in my classroom." I don't know where to put my eyes. I blame bloody Channel 4, but who knew she was awake?

"I'm so sorry, I think she was nervous," is all I can muster. Carlton just dare not speak. He's transfixed by Mrs Crecher, he's gone back in time to infant school and looks like the boy who has just pissed his pants.

We stand up to leave. In the corner are two children who look like butter wouldn't melt. Carlton and I walk towards our children, waiting to see what the other does first, but I know it's probably for me to show the way. I walk up to Davina, but before I get anywhere near she sticks out her tongue and runs off. I smile back.

"I'm going to count to three, Davina, and you must come straight back."

When I'm at two and three quarters, I decide to change tack. Lionel and Carlton are getting their coats on. I tell Davina the school is going to close and she will spend the night here… nothing…

"Without Mr Ted Ted."

A face appears. My little monster cannot sleep without Mr Ted Ted. *Thank you, Mr Ted Ted.* We leave. The playground is empty except for Carlton and Lionel. We walk back to the car in silence. Even the children are quiet. I reach the car and remove the parking ticket. Carlton tells me he can take care of that messy bob if I need him to. *Rude*, I chunter to myself. It's not a bob, it's a grow back. The bloody baby absorbed all my hair and grew it on her head and body. I think I'm the only mother who gave birth to a silverback!

Each morning is the same saga. I really try to get up early to make myself look presentable. In fact, one morning I went the full monty. I even put on eye shadow and mascara. At 6.30 a.m. I looked presentable. Problem was, I fell asleep on the settee and so by 8.30 a.m., I looked like something a cat had dragged through the hedge backwards! Accepting your place in the playground is just one hurdle. There are many more; for example, choosing an appropriate outfit for your child on World Book Day. The toffee cake making brigade are surrounded by mini 'Where's Wallys' and 'Harry Potters'. Sending Davina dressed as High Heeled Moo Cow (from *Moo-Cow-Kung-Fu-Cow*) did not go down well. I thought it would be unique, make her stand out. However, when she came home crying because everyone had laughed at her and Lionel had tried to milk her, I decided next year she would be Red Riding Hood, before she is permanently scarred.

The fear at the end of the day never goes. Will I be summoned today? If I don't make eye contact with Mrs

Crecher, she may forget and I may be able to grab my little darling and make a quick getaway, I think. But it never works, her eyes burn into the back of my head. I know she is glaring. When I take a quick swiping glance, she sees me and out comes the finger. Oh crap, here we go again.

Chapter Two
The Gym

I've started to reclaim my life. There are now suddenly gaps in the day when I think, *I'm ready to do something else right now.* My caesarean scar, some five years on, has healed, and so I decide it's time to hit the gym. I check out the local ones, but soon realise everyone I know goes there so I need to look further afield. The one thirty minutes' drive fence to door is perfect. Perfect, bugger me, it has movies and popcorn nights on a Friday for the kids with trained child professional people. There's even a soft play area and a Costa. (And I may have noticed the Pinot Grigio!). So here it is. The gym, or family wellbeing centre as they call it these days. Or, as Pete would say, "Rob you blind and make you work for it club."

So this is when my fantasy of looking like a pin up model and doing a shoot in FHM Magazine about how I lost the baby weight and turned into this gorgeous creature fails. That first session around the gym when a trainer called Faith, who looks like she can drag a fleet of cars on her back, faces me and tells me to press. *Press?* Isn't that something to do with the papers? What are these heavy things you've stuck at the end, they are hindering my ability to lift my arm, let alone press. She then whips me up in some kind of machine, strapping my arms as far apart from my body as humanly possible, so that it feels like they are no longer attached.

"Pull," shouts the vicious bitch. I pull, but nothing moves except that burning feeling in the pit of my stomach like I'm about to vomit, and my arms that were once attached are now throbbing. I leave the gym. My first fifteen minute introduction did not go well. I walk down the stairs like a German Storm Trooper. My knees no longer bend, I feel a little broken. I decide I need a swim. Being a member of a club like this, I can do that. I can do the gym and swim as I am a guru of all things fitness like. I get my costume out, which I haven't worn in over seven years. Surely my body cannot have changed that much? I confidently slip it on, without first checking in the mirror. There's a tightness, but that's expected, I've had a baby. I'm sure it will be fine. It's only when I hit the water that I realise my costume never used to have the G-string effect. In fact, definitely not, it was one of the M&S hold-you-in-the-arse type costumes. In addition to this, my breasts have taken up position outside the deliberate cup holder for my once perfect B cup boobs. *What is going on?* Bloody washing machine. Shrinks everything. After one length, I decide that swimming is not happening today. It is difficult to swim with just one hand (the other keeps pulling out my costume from between my arse cheeks). Maybe a hot steam or sauna instead. I get out of the pool and swear I hear a cackling sound. Is someone laughing? I enter the sauna. It's busy. No one utters a word. I take a step up to the highest bench, just passing some thirty-something body building type. He's clearly pretending not to look. I can't quite read his face; is he smiling or smirking? As I climb up I swear I hear a retching sound. I lay back, satisfied that all is right in the world. I hear the door open and a "holy shit", and then the door shuts. Too hot for some – pah! After twenty minutes, I walk out. At peace with my inner soul. I swagger past the pool. They all look. I think they are impressed, spending that long in the sauna. As I enter the changing room, I pass a few mirrors. I dare to take a glance. *What the chuff!* Before me is a fat bird wearing a mankini. There are boobs popping out either side, arse cheeks on display, and what looks like everything has been cooked to overkill. *It can't be me,* I promise myself. I look again to see if it's actually someone else, but then I recognise the nose, the mole just to the left and that spot on the upper lip that I think is a spot but it's been there an awfully long time (I should probably get it checked). If you ever wondered what Nanny McPhee and Jabba the Hutt's love child looks like, this would be a close replica.

So I swear to myself I won't step a foot in that gym or pool again, for at least, well, until I've lost half my body weight. However, given Pete has paid six months upfront, I have to come here and do something, and, somehow, drinking Caramel Frappuccino's isn't going to help. I wander around the gym and see a class. A class where everyone is just stood lifting weights. I keep watching to see if they are going to burst into some kind of run, but no. They stand still. In fact, they don't leave the spot except when their legs go backwards to do press-ups. They are selecting their own weights. Now here is a class I can do. I sign up immediately – it's called Body Pump. Rock on. Roll on Tuesday.

It's Tuesday, I take Davina to school in my gym kit. Apparently even when they are only five, you can be an embarrassment to your child. She won't walk with me, she says I look like one of the M&M's off the advert on telly. I walk up to my new friend, Carlton. He's looking a bit weary today. He tells me Lionel refused to sleep last night. Instead he ran around the house, screaming, "I'm Superman," wearing just his underpants. Poor Carlton, he is still adjusting to parenthood. So, after the bell rings and I've shoved my little darling through the door, holding it closed and then making a run for it – a dump and run is the term I like to use – it's time to face my class.

I arrive in good time. I go and sit outside the studio, waiting for the previous class to finish. As the time draws nearer, no-one else arrives. I become a little concerned that it's only going to be the instructor and me. I can't do that. There will be nowhere to hide! I was planning on taking a position at the back. When the last class finishes, I then realise that everyone is actually staying for the next class, bloody carrot-eating, body-loving stiffs. I am forced to walk into the studio on my own. I walk up to the instructor, who is about 5ft2 but built like Arnold Schwarzenegger. I have to identify myself as the newbie. "Oh, you are new," she announces over the microphone. Everyone stares. She helps set me up, at the front, bitch. She waits until I take off my jumper before she gets the weights. She then hands me two flat looking things that look like pancakes. *I can lift more than that*, I think to myself. "I wouldn't recommend going any heavier for a while."

The music starts. "Embrace your core," she says. What does that mean? Am I supposed to give myself a hug? I complete the warm up, it's not actually that bad. I turn to my side to give the person next to me a nod of approval but she won't make eye contact. I look at her weight bar. She's loading up ready for the next track. It's got three five-kilo weights on each end. She's only 4ft8; if she lifts that she will fall through the ceiling. With precision, she lifts the bar and places it on the meaty part of her back. "Show off," I chunter to myself.

First track, squats. "Stick that bootie back, ladies," shouts the instructor, who I now know is called Jade. My bootie is stuck back, it's always like that. "Knees over your middle toe." How the chuff do you do that, then? I lean forward and try to bend over my toes. Jade squats over to me. She sticks her perfectly tight arse in my face in an attempt to show me how to squat. I try to copy her and feel a huge amount of sympathy for the poor girl behind me. As I try to mirror her, I feel the most incredible pain in my thighs, arse, and calves. *Fucking hell*, I want to scream. "Come on, ladies, only another two hundred to go." *You've got to be kidding me.* I can't squat another two hundred times. Just when I think it cannot get any worse, she makes us stay low and bounce. I let out a fart and just pray no one heard. I don't really care, I have bigger things to worry about than a fart, the biggest being trying not to shit myself or vomit. It's over.

Jade squats over to the sound system to press pause. Excellent. We get a break now but then more music. Everyone in the room except me is lying on their back with their bar in the air. Without trying to make too much of a scene, I lay back on my bench and struggle to lift the bar above my head. This is then followed by about four minutes of absolute torture. My chest is about to pop out, my arms are shaking so much that I'm worried I am going to drop the bar on my head, or worse still, the wobbly left side will land on Jade's head.

Now that I've actually lost the ability to use my arms and legs, the rest of the class goes by in a blur. I accept defeat. I use every opportunity I can to get out of doing the exercise: I sneeze, blow my nose, pretend there is something in my eye, click my knees, rub my back, anything to help pass those torturous minutes of pain I am putting myself through. At the end, everyone claps. Why? What is there to clap about? I want to die. Are they clapping because they didn't shit their pants or vomit? I personally want to go up to Jade and punch her in the face. As I start to put my things away, I see the pool of sweat on the floor. Everyone is making a deliberate point of stepping around it. It's not that big, just a small puddle. Jade hands me some paper towels, far more than is actually needed to mop it up, but I use them all anyway.

I leave the class feeling a little smug as I see the people sat on the bench outside waiting for their class. They are all about sixty plus, with mats under their arms. Ahh, it's pilates. Maybe that would have been better for me, what with my back, knee, etc. As I walk with the others, they are all chatting in their little groups. I feel as though I should now belong, having completed my first pump, and then one of them actually talks to me. "You won't be able to walk tomorrow," she says in a slightly unfriendly tone. "Never mind tomorrow, I can't walk now," I say, trying to strike up a conversation. She ignores me and carries on talking to her equally toned friend, whose biceps look like they are going to pop any minute. I get to the top of the stairs and know this is going to be a challenge. Never mind the Storm Trooper walk, I can't actually raise my leg at all. I take it slowly. With each step I let out a little cry. It's like I'm walking on glass. Ooh, the pain. I gather my stuff up from the changing room. I'm not showering here. I'm not sure I will actually be able to undress and dress myself. As I leave the gym, the nice guy behind the desk says bye and for some reason, for some completely bizarre reason, I find myself booking back in to next week's class.

The next morning I actually cannot move. My legs hurt to touch. I nudge Pete and tell him he will have to take Davina to school today. I cannot get out of bed. By lunchtime and 500mg of ibuprofen later, I start to get some feeling back. After coming out of the shower, I take a quick sneak peak in the mirror to see if my body is black and blue. It isn't, but what I do notice, and it takes me completely by surprise, is some very slight definition in my legs. They are no longer completely like tree trunks – there is a hint of some muscle poking through. My shoulders too. I turn to the side – whoa! Okay, let's not get carried away. I'm impressed. If after just one class I see this, imagine what I will look like after ten, or even one hundred. I am so pleased I decide to eat the last Danish swirl to celebrate. I lay out those jeans that once fitted me so well but now I cannot get up past my ankle. "One day, my friend," I tell my skinny jeans. "We will be together again soon."

Chapter Three
Pete's 40th

So, it's Pete's 40th birthday. He doesn't want a big to do, just something quiet and low key. Bugger that, I say. I've been going to the gym now for the past eight weeks and have dropped a dress size. No, we are going to have a party, a big party, something I can invite all my friends to and finally get my legs out for. This is what I need, something to look forward to. Since Pete is the quiet, stand at the back of the room type, I decide the perfect way to humiliate him is to make it a fancy dress party. After scouring the internet, our costumes are ordered. He's Captain America and I am a bumblebee. Now for the invitations. After looking through the various photo albums, I realise I don't actually have any pictures of Pete from when he was a baby. Bollocks. This means I've got to call his mother. Oh crap. There is no such thing as quick conversation with Pete's mother. I may as well write off the day, as this going to be a long one, particularly as I haven't seen the outlaws for almost two months. After talking myself out of a large glass of gin, I sit down with a coffee and dial. The phone rings...

"243890, Raynard residence."

"Hi, Carol, it's Jess."

"Hello, hello."

"I've got it, John, put the phone down."

"Who is it?"

"It's Jess."

"Jess who?"

"Our Jess."

"We don't have a Jess."

"Pete's Jess."

Oh, for God's sake, I say to myself.

"Oh, that Jess. Hi, Jess."

"Hi, John."

"Everything okay?"

"Yes, fine, thank you. Well, you know, my knee is still playing up and I can't see properly out of my left eye, but apart from that we are hunky dory."

"Put the phone down, John," snaps Carol.

"Righto, will do, but can I have cup of tea and some of that chocolate cake you made?"

"Fine."

John goes. One down. Ninety minutes later, I put the phone down. The earpiece is sticky and has my blusher welded to it. We've covered every topic of conversation imaginable. Of course, asking for a picture of their beloved and only child, Pete, means we go through the entire album from one day old up to his eleventh birthday. There were tears and laughter, none from me, well, except when I farted really loudly whilst having a wee. When Carol asked what it was, I told her I didn't hear anything, must be a glitch in their line. The conversation only ended because I agreed to go over for dinner a week on Sunday, anything to shut her up and stop the incessant chatter. She's promised to post some photos for the invites, which, by the way, means I have to invite them to the party, especially since John owns his own Viking costume.

Within a few days, a perfectly written envelope lands on our doorstep. As promised, photos of the golden boy. On a beautifully written piece of note paper, with their address typed in black font at the top, is a message from my mother in law. "Here are some of the best ones. Do please be careful with them, they are our only copy and we would not them to get spoilt. Please bring them back when you are done with them (notice the words "bring back", another attempt to cast her web around me). If you can, also bring the casserole dish back we lent you for Davina's 3rd birthday." Crap, I'd hoped they had forgotten.

The invites are done, thanks to Truprint. Isn't t'internet bloody brilliant? How we ever managed to get anything done before is amazing. I remember the days I used to have to sit and write out each of my party invites on a bit of crappy looking paper with badly drawn balloons and a mouse eating cake on it. Now, it's a high gloss picture of Pete aged approximately three years old, sat in the sea at Scarborough with his tinky winky out. All the details are printed on the front and there's even a tear off slip for RSVP.

The idea of the party starts small, just a few friends, fancy dress, nothing flash, but I soon realise I've invited over fifty people. Fifty people won't fit in our house and even if they did, I wouldn't want fifty people in our house: that could be potentially over four hundred wees in one night. That's a lot of piss to mop up off the floor. No, I'll just have to hire a marquee. Not an expensive one like you have at a wedding, a cheaper looking thing. A few calls later and Carl and Stan from Just Pop it Up are booked. It was a bit more expensive than I thought it would be, but they are throwing in lights, chairs and tables. Therefore, £800 really isn't that bad.

The costumes have arrived but I decide it's probably best not to let Pete know just yet, it will only give him something else to moan about. I try on the bumble bee costume. It's a bit tight and I really cannot bend down without flashing my bloomers, but in another couple of weeks and after several more pump classes, it will be a perfect fit, I might just need to lower the wings slightly to cover my arse, that's all.

It's the week before the party. It's time to tell Pete it's more than just a few friends and nibbles. After all, there will be a bloody great marquee in the garden in a couple of days. "So, Peter," I say whilst dishing out his favourite homemade shepherd's pie, "there's been a slight change of plan for your birthday." Pete looks at me. "Well, you see, of course Faye, Ian, Matt and Leigh, Lou and Frank are coming, and you can't invite them without inviting Claire and Dave, Jerry and Julie and Jase and Lisa, and then, you see, that then led to the Beverley crowd, and Becky and Martin wanted to come with Tina and Russell."

"So what you're saying is, it's no longer a small gathering. That's okay, I'm just glad it's at home, but we will have to just have prosecco and not champagne.

Shit, I've ordered thirty bottles of champagne, I think to myself. "Well, about it being at home." He gives me that look. "It's still at home, just in the garden that's all, sort of in a marquee, but not a posh one."

"Jesus wept, Jess. I told you I didn't want anything flash."

"It won't be flash, I promise. I went for the cheap white tablecloths, as opposed to the double layered blue and white, and I won't be doing big table displays."

"How much has that cost?"

"Oh, you don't need to worry about that, it's your birthday." I make a mental note to keep the credit card bill hidden for the next few months, certainly until the party has passed – by then he won't care, as he will have had such an awesome time.

"So, how many?"

"Well, so far fifty-eight have confirmed."

"Fifty-eight." He's stopped eating now. Now I know I'm in trouble. "What we going to feed them?"

"I've taken care of all that. We are having a hog roast, it's cheap and we only need baps and sauces." I can tell that he's a little chuffed about that. Most men like the idea of a large piece of meat cooking in their garden. Something to do with their inner caveman.

"Anything else I should know about MY birthday?"

"Well, the band will only play until twelve, they can't play much later as they get tired. Raging Rockers is quite a misrepresentation." His hands are covering his face now. "Oh and it's, erm, well, it's fancy dress.

"No, Jess." He's not amused.

"Afraid so, the invites have gone out saying it's fancy dress."

"Well I'm not getting dressed up, it's my birthday and I don't have to." I decide not to mention at this particular point about the Captain America costume. I think he needs some time.

It's the party, everyone is arriving. Pete is stood, unamused, in his Captain America costume, greeting people as they arrive. It cost me four blowjobs to get him to wear it but it was worth it, he looks like a true super hero. It's amazing the effort people go to at such parties. We have Lawrence of Arabia, the marshmallow man from Ghostbusters, there was almost the entire cast of The Wizard of Oz, including Toto. My personal favourite, however, was the giant sperm. It took me a while to work it out. Pete's mum still thinks it's the plasticine Morph from Tony Hart. (Google it if you are too young).

I really didn't go over the top with the decorations, just a few flower displays for each table. Well, okay, fifteen to be exact, and of course the 40th sprinkle things you scatter on the table next to the glass tea light holders. Well, lighting is very important. You can't skimp on things like that. Okay, so perhaps the glass holders didn't need to have that cracked glass effect, which cost an extra £5.00 each, but the effect was worth it. However, the best purchase was the hiring of the portable toilet. No piss stains to wipe up in the morning.

It's a cracking night. Of course, I drink far too much and, since it's our party, I can take possession of the microphone from the band I paid for and sing my heart out with my bestie, Faye. At the end of the night, I lay out flat on the bed, fully clothed of course, make up still on. I wake up to the sound of Auntie Janet ringing the doorbell, returning our child. One of us needs to get up and let her in. However, Pete is snoring his head off so it's left to me. I stagger down the stairs and catch a glimpse of myself in the mirror. I look like a bumble bee that flew into the car windscreen. It's really not a good look and Auntie Janet won't be amused, hence why Auntie Janet wasn't invited to the party. She doesn't do parties, which is exactly why she is the perfect babysitter.

As I open the door, Davina lets out a little scream. "Mummy, what happened to you?"

"Mummy's been playing dress up, darling." Davina runs off into the lounge and puts on the telly. I lean in to give Auntie Janet a kiss but she pulls back; the stench of stale alcohol is lingering and my breath smells like something crawled in there and died. I make Auntie Janet a coffee and an extra strong one for myself. As I start talking about the previous night, I realise that I am actually still pissed. I know this because I stand up, showing Auntie Janet how I did that amazing bee dance where I spun like this with my wings and then, stop it. I am going to vomit.

After twenty minutes of explaining everything Davina did, including the poop in her pants, Auntie Janet leaves. I then question whether it is acceptable to leave our five-year-old in front of the telly with a tube of smarties and the promise of a new toy and go back to bed? Probably not. Instead, I go upstairs and make as much as noise as possible getting changed out of my bumble bee outfit so that Pete wakes up and realises I've been up. "Davina is downstairs."

He farts, scratches his arse and pats the bed. "Since she's downstairs, fancy a quickie?" This is typical Pete. I'm still pissed and my hangover hasn't kicked in yet, and this is his way of dealing with the morning after. I think he thinks that if you have sex you will avoid the hangover. Well, if he's up for sex, he's up for looking after the child.

"Well, since your up, you can go see to Davina," I say as I sidle back into bed. He lays there, thinking I am joking. I turn to the side to prove I'm not. He feels my arse and I can almost hear the comment in his head, "Ohh, that's shrunk a bit." Secretly pleased but without any chance of sex, I grab the duvet and shove it over my head to prove I mean business. He stomps out of bed. Finally, he gets the message.

Chapter Four
Girlie Day

As every girl, woman, beast knows, there is nothing you benefit more from in life than being with your girlfriends. I love my husband and my child, but nothing beats girlie time. It's a special thing, particularly with close friends. They are the tonic to my gin, the lemon to my tequila, the prawn in my paella, you get the gist. If life involved no girlie days, what a very dull life it would be. Today's gathering is just a lunch. I tell myself this, but I know, as does Pete, that it actually is an all-day drinking binge session which will involve me falling through the door at some ungodly hour, puking up my guts and spending the entire next day in bed swearing that it was either something I ate or that someone spiked my drink. However I try to justify my state and regardless of all the promises I make that it's just a day thing, no biggy, it's all complete bollocks. I am going out and will be getting shit faced.

The what to wear saga. So I've lost the weight and I can actually fit into most of my pre-pregnancy clothes. The problem is, my pre-pregnancy clothes were bought in my twenties. The dresses are just that little bit too short to go unnoticed, and not in a good way, because although I've lost the weight, there is still that dimple effect sitting just under my arse cheeks. In addition to the shortness of the dresses, there is also the problem of the tightness of the tops. Again, despite losing the weight, these tops cling to me like spandex in a heatwave. They are unforgiving and, I'm sorry, Marks & Spencers, but your hold-you-in pants, tights, vests, all in one just does not cut it. Only if I actually wear something from the ankle to the neck about three sizes too small will I actually be fully sucked in, and even then I will have about six double chins (well, it has to go somewhere). My options are limited. I can put on my skinny jeans, but unless I opt for that jumper with the pattern, I am buggered. Oh, but hang on, there is that one dress, that little number that makes my tits look huge, has a massive belt which actually hides my waist and a skirt that hangs and floats a good respectable amount above the knee, enough to show some thigh but not so much that the Emmental cheese type legs are shown. This is it. I put it on. I don't even need tights and it doesn't matter if I opt for G-string or full briefs as no-one will be seeing through this. Of course, I opt for G-string because I just so can right now.

Shoes are never a problem. I slip on those wedges because, let's face it, wedges rock. They go with anything, except an all in one leotard, but that's another story! I am done. I check myself out, not bad, not bad. I grab that little handbag that I can carry under my arm pit. There is just my purse, phone, lipstick and keys in there. The sheer delight of being able to carry a bag that doesn't weigh you down so you walk like Quasimodo is an absolute luxury. Although it actually makes me a little panicked. *Will I forget it?* There is always that chance, but that is why Pete has the locksmith's number on speed dial.

The next task is deciding how much money I need. Now, if I were to be honest here, and truly honest, I know I will be getting no change from £100.00, and that isn't including my taxi fare home. However, for some reason, we woman believe that if we only take out £50.00, we will only actually spend £50.00. Well, that's just crap, because, as we all know, out comes the card. It doesn't count when I pay by card so I can be as generous as I like. No money actually exchanges hands.

So here I am, all set to go. I go downstairs and Pete gives me the once over. Now, one of two things happens here, he either immediately starts sulking, which is clearly a sign that I look hot, OR he tells me to have a good time and say "Hi" to the girls. The latter occurs today. But then again, it is only a lunch time meeting, so I can't get dressed up as a hottie today, but, deep down, I am a little pissed he's happy for me to go out.

I sneak out without Davina noticing. It's on a need to know basis. Does she need to know mummy is going out? Yes. Does she need to know at this point that I am leaving the house? No. Can she find out once I have gone? Yes. Will she kick off? Yes. Will Daddy feed her with chocolate and let her watch Frozen fifteen times? Yes.

I am in the car, on my own. Wow. That feels good. Capital FM goes straight on the stereo. I have absolutely no idea who is playing, but it sounds brilliant. I sing my head off without knowing a single word – it does not matter because there is no-one in the car to challenge me. As I pull up outside my bestie's house, I take a quick look in the rear view mirror because, deep down, as much as I love her, I've got to try look better than her. This can be quite a challenge, because I don't hang around with fugglies – which is a massive error of judgment on my part, as then I would always be the fairest of them all. I knock on the door. Ian answers. "She's still getting ready." Of course she is, she's always late, but that's fine. Ian looks pissed off. *Bollocks*, I say to myself. *She must look great.* And then it happens, she walks down the stairs wearing a tight body con dress that curves in all the right places. Those Kurt Geiger heels make her look like she's 6ft5 and that leopard print clutch bag just pulls it all together. *Bitch.* Whilst I longingly look at my friend and try to decide if she really has had a spray tan for this 'girlie luncheon', or whether it has been particularly sunny in Newton on Derwent, I am reminded of my own failings as her two perfect blonde-haired blue-eyed children come through to give me a hug. Bless them. There's only eleven months between them, the last being eleven months old. Just another reminder that actually, five years on, I'm really not doing as well as I should.

I give Faye a huge squeeze and tell her she looks gorgeous, and she does and I can forgive her for it because she's my bestie. Just as we are about to leave the house, Ian strides over to ask Faye if she has enough money. Now, sorry, guys, but when you do this, you are doing this to try and have a dig and pick a little fight, to make us feel guilty for going out. Raise the subject of money at the point where we leave, why don't you? Obviously, this is a perfectly apt time to discuss money, just as we are going out the door. It doesn't work, there will be no guilt from us: we deserve this.

We are in the car heading into town. (The car is being dumped and collected the next day.) We arrive at the restaurant, The Inn in the City. It's a classy place but, then, we are classy girls, for now! And there they are, the girlies. They have clearly all been here for some time – I blame Faye. The greetings start. We hug and kiss like we've not seen each other in a decade. (It was actually only three weeks ago at Evie's 4th birthday party, but that's beside the point.) Then Freya does that thing that Freya does at every meeting; she gets out her camera and starts with the photos. At the time, I always get pretty arsey because I just want to chat and get drunk but actually, the next day, I am really grateful, particularly because she has great editing software and always sends photos that make me look fantastic.

Now, for some reason, when I am out with the girls, I decide that despite being absolutely starving because I've only had a banana for breakfast (I didn't want my stomach to inflate), I am going to have a salad. What I actually really fancy is the steak pie with homemade chips presented in a copper pan, but for some reason, I decide a salad is all I need. Salad and prosecco please. Side orders – olives! Like they will do any good! Who has ever heard anyone say "Thank God I had some olives last night or else I would have been in a right mess today"?

As my food arrives, I look about the table. Faye has ordered the steak Diane and has chips – really, really good chips – in a copper pan, Freya has sea bass served with dill and caper new potatoes, Lou has the goat cheese and aubergine cheesecake and Kayleigh has the lamb shank with mint sauce and roasted root vegetables. Okay, so it is just me who has the salad, that's fine, I just won't drink as much.

As the luncheon progresses, we laugh – oh boy do we laugh. Suddenly, everything is funny. Placing a black straw in between your nose and lip to look like a moustache is funny stuff. Any concern for money is out the window. "Another two bottles of prosecco," I shout to the waiter. When I see people turning and looking at us, I believe it is admiration, admiration for being such a good looking group of girls having a fab day out. The fact that we are properly shouting at one another has nothing to do with it. When the lovely young waiter suggests we sit outside on the terrace because the sun is out, we genuinely believe he's looking out for our interests. The fact we should just go and leave our drinks, he will bring them out, is just really excellent customer service.

Now here comes that part in the day where it's getting close to tea time. We've been out for a good four and a half hours. I am in that happy, pissed state, but not too pissed that there is any chance of regurgitating my food at this juncture. Now the **sensible** thing to do (I've highlighted it as a reminder to look that word up in the Oxford dictionary), would be to get the last bus home or even call Pete to pick me up as he said he would provided its before six p.m. Freya, Lou and Kayleigh are all making their arrangements to head home and just at the point where I start thinking about picking up my phone, Faye looks at me. She has those pleading eyes, like the eyes from Puss in Boots in *Shrek* – in fact, I think she's purring. And so it starts, my bestie, purring at me. It takes all of about a millisecond to agree to stay out and not go home just yet. But I have conditions. My conditions are that I need to eat more food at some point in the evening, and that does not mean a dirty kebab on the way home. It means, the two of us sitting down somewhere and sharing a pizza perhaps. Of course, she agrees. She would agree to anything right now.

As everyone gets up to leave, we decide it's time to go try somewhere new, but we first head to the bathroom. As I reapply my lipstick in the mirror, I watch Faye checking herself out in the full length mirror. She looks super-hot, I look like a frumpy mummy. This outfit does not reveal the months of hard work at fat fighters and selling every muscle to the body pump gym goddess. No, this will not do. I tell Faye that before we are going anywhere else, we need to go shopping, I need something new to wear: since we are heading into the ;evening' time, it's only right I have 'evening' wear. I check the 'emergency' credit card is still in my wallet and has not been removed by Pete; phew, it's still there.

After calling Pete and doing my best impersonation of a sober person (I think he actually bought it), we head to the most expensive department store in York. We could have gone to one of the cheap shops where you wear an outfit once, twice at best, then bin it or use it as duster but no, this is a special day with my special friend and therefore I need to look that little bit extra special. I decide that the short leather skirt and skintight cotton vest with a chain around the collar is definitely the right look for the evening. The skirt is actually in the sale and a real bargain at £160.00, reduced from £210.00. I mean, I know there isn't actually much leather to it, but it's a nice cut and Pete will like it. The top, at £90.00, well, it just goes so well and when I suck in, I've no belly at all. It's actually flattering, I'm sure I will wear it loads.

Thankfully, I don't need to buy shoes because, as I say, wedges go with anything. After paying for my goods, I walk back into the changing room to get changed. Faye has gone missing. She's somewhere in Woman's Wear but I am not sure where. I just hope she hasn't decided to chat up one of the mannequins like she did in Harvey Nicks last Christmas. When she started rubbing his pants, security suggested we leave quietly or be escorted out.

As I am about to leave the changing room, I give myself one final look over. My outfit but looks great, my hair is okay but oh, my face, I need more than just lipstick here. It won't do. Thank goodness we are in a department store. After finding Faye, who's trying on over the knee leather stiletto boots, gliding her hands up and down them, I convince her we need to head back downstairs. I need a makeover. Faye is game. We head downstairs and look around. Oh boy, which to choose? Who looks most tolerant? We opt for Christian Dior. As we swagger up to the lady, who looks old enough to be our mother but aiming for twenty years younger, I tell her she needs to "do something with this," circling my entire face. She calls for back up. Faye and I are seated side by side so the work can begin. The polite conversation commences. "Are you out on a special occasion?"

"I've just had a baby," I find myself saying.

"Oh," goes the gooey mother type, "how old?"

"Five, er, five months."

"Wow, you look amazing," she replies. It would be a very dull story to say it's taken five years for me to start getting my life back.

After twenty five minutes, which, by the way, is really pissing me off as I desperately need a drink, I am presented with the new me. Hmmm. I look like a younger version of the Dior counter lady. That really was not the look I was going for. I look at Faye and she looks the same as me, except her lipstick is called Very Plum, mine is Very Berry. Sod it. We haven't the time or the inclination to go through it again. I buy all the products – I have to. It would be rude not to. With little change from £150.00, we hit the street. This is it, we are ready for it. The evening is ours. Just me and Faye, two hot chicks out on the town. We are just like everyone else on a Saturday tea time, casually walking through the streets of York. *Bollocks, I'm on the ground, why do they have to have some many cobbled roads?*

We choose a bar that has 'Happy Hour' written on the board outside. I can't drink anymore prosecco: a) I can't afford it, especially now, and b) my mouth keeps drying up and I'm burping prosecco bubbles. Cocktails seems sensible, a mixture of fruit and alcohol, that will help me stay compos mentis, right? Wrong. Drinking cocktails after a shit load of prosecco is like swallowing the worm at the bottom of the tequila bottle. It all feels fine for about the first half hour and then, bang – I'm gone. A typical sign for me is when my farts really stink bad, and I mean bad. It's a putrid, lingering stench from the bog of stinky fart pit. I believe that because there are men around, the farts can easily be assigned to one of them, but the reality is that farty putrid smell lingers with me. Wherever I go, it goes. There is no getting anyway from it. Faye doesn't notice it because she's dropped a similar number herself. It's at this point usually in an evening when the young twenty year old lads decide they want to chat us up. Whether this is because they know that stench so well because they smell similar, perhaps students, or because they still like the idea of shagging Stifler's Mum (*American Pie*), who knows, however they come on strong and a bit sexy, I think. Perhaps if they could stand still, I could have a better look.

I am at that barrier where I know if I caught Pete gyrating his arse up against a twenty something like I am doing right now that I would cut off his bollocks and blend them, but somehow because it's me and I have no intention of doing anything with this boy, it's okay. I gyrate until my knees are touching the ground, because I can now do that. This is then followed by a conversation asking the twenty something to guess how old I am. When he guesses two years older than I actually am, I have to decide whether to agree that this is my age or go two years above, to prove I look younger. The older, look younger wins all the time.

After we manage to pull ourselves away from the rampant twenty somethings, we decide we perhaps need to head to a bar filled with people more our age group. We head to AllBarOne. The downside of a bar like this is that they won't serve us. They take one look at us and say they are sorry but they cannot serve us. We now have to question whether or not it's time to call it a day, or try for another bar. Taking one look at Faye, who is propping herself up against the coat stand, I decide it's time to call it a day. Damn, I've only been wearing my new outfit for approximately ninety minutes.

Somehow, I manage to get home. The next day is like a gorilla has been in my room and beaten me with my handbag. It hurts so much I can feel a pulse throbbing. I actually have to touch my head to see if I can feel the boom boom. I look at the clock and just in front is a cold cup of tea and two paracetamol. Bless Pete. He's a good man, really. It's 10.30. It can't be. Surely the clocks are wrong, I've only been asleep for about three hours. I know if I sleep anymore, I really am taking the piss, since I will have been out for coming up to almost twenty four hours. I get out of bed but realise I am naked. How did that happen? Well, I do hate it when I get caught up in my nightie. I must have decided to go without to avoid any disturbed sleep – see, I can't have been that pissed. Then again, how did I get home??

I go downstairs. Davina is in the lounge. *Jungle Book* is on and she's playing with her toy kitchen. "Morning, sweetheart," is all I can muster. I go into the kitchen. Pete is there. He's sat at the kitchen table reading the paper. He's brewed some fresh coffee and the toaster pops. I gag. For some reason the smell of toast smells like prosecco. It's not good. *Pull yourself together*, I tell myself. I have to maintain the 'I wasn't too pissed' last night moment. I try to hide the fact I've just vomited in my mouth slightly. I get a large glass of water and neck it in one. I then put the kettle on, pretending I can manage a cup of tea. Pete still hasn't said anything at this point. In fact, a good few minutes pass and he's still not said anything. I pour the tea, knowing fine well I can't drink it. I am starting to feel a little brave now. "Aren't you going to ask if I had a good day?" Silence. Pete crunches on his toast and slurps his coffee. Cocky bastard.

"I don't think there isn't anything I don't know about your whole day out with the girls." Note, 'whole day' – oh boy, he's pissed. "I was particularly interested in the twenty year olds you and Faye were chatting to. You know, the ones that were amazed at how good you look and thought you were twenty eight, how they said they wished they had a girlfriend with a body like yours. I was even more interested to hear all about your shopping trip to Spenwicks and the bargains you got. I cannot wait for you to wear that leather skirt with stockings for me, like you promised." Gulp. "I've spoken to Ian and he says he found Faye asleep in the downstairs toilet. He was worried sick." Oh shit, he's pissed, he's even worse than pissed, he's been conversing with Ian. That's never a good sign. And then it starts, the lecture. The fact we are putting ourselves at risk getting into that state. The concern for our wellbeing. I know they mean it and they are probably right, but still, I'm not a child. I know what I'm doing, sort of. (I just need to remember how I got home.) The good thing about Pete is that he always goes on that bit too much; rather than give a short sharp bollocking, he drags it out, and that's his downfall. If he didn't go on quite so much, I would remain sheepish, apologise, hug him and swear never to do it again. However, because he has gone on and on and on, I end up getting really pissed off. It then turns into a 'Who the fuck are you, the hangover police?' type argument. The day goes by, it's never a good one. Pete is walking about feeling smug, I feel like crap. But I know that tomorrow I will feel better and Pete can come down from his moral high ground.

Chapter Five
It's Christmas

If you don't have children, firstly, why the hell are you reading this book? (Was it stuck on the shelf in the doctor's surgery and are you actually still waiting to see the doctor?). As every parent knows, this is a magical time. It's that time where you over indulge with everything: presents, decorations, food, Christmas jumpers. For some reason, despite never buying them at any other time in the year, I decide I need to have at least two massive tubs of Quality Street chocolates and they need to be put out in little bowls around the house, including nuts. Why do we buy nuts at Christmas? What is it about nuts that just completes Christmas? They too go out in little bowls dotted around the house and every time I walk past, I grab a chocolate and a pile of nuts. This usually results in putting on a stone the week before Christmas. In spite of all this, Christmas is just not Christmas unless there is a child in the house, someone much younger than Pete, preferably aged with one numeric number.

At age five, the little darlings really know what's going on. They know who Santa is and what he is going to do. Thankfully, they still know and believe in the "Santa cam". You know, the alarm sets in the corner of each room. Every time it flashes when Davina walks into a room, I tell her it's just Santa checking in. It took a bit of getting used to, as I would often find her sat chatting to the corner of the ceiling. However, then I explained it's only a one way thing, Santa can see and hear EVERYTHING, but he cannot hear you. So when she has deliberately coloured in the flower pattern of my Laura Ashley wallpaper, it is no good saying "Sorrwee, Santa." He can't hear you! "Actions, Davina, have consequences. Don't do it and no sorrwee is required!"

Now if you are anything like me, you leave Christmas shopping right until the last minute. I work better under pressure. I spend more because I can't be as selective and go hunting for bargains, I just see something I like and buy it. I don't contemplate how many scarves Auntie Janet actually has, I just buy it because I have to, there are only seven days until Christmas. The only person I do buy in advance for is Davina. My childhood Christmasses were all about quantity, not quality. Don't get me wrong, I got some quality items – the original Peaches and Cream Barbie doll was treasured for many years – but the excitement for me was seeing sacks full of presents. My parents would spend hours wrapping up individual items. I could spend a good hour just opening rubbers (the rubbing out pencil types!). That feeling when you walk downstairs and see just how much Santa loves you is priceless. So it's a tradition I like to continue in our house. The problem is, now with the internet and the likes of Groupon, I get really carried away. When I see a talking budgie in a cage that originally cost £30.00 but today is only £8.00, I feel the need to buy it, and since I generally get at least two to three emails a day from Groupon, the likes of the budgie and other bargains soon mounts. By the end of Christmas, I am on first name terms with my Hermes delivery man. I know that his wife, Beryl, is awaiting a hip operation and he is just earning some extra cash so he can take some time off with her when she has the op.

The next problem, for me anyway, is having bought all these many bargains, I need to store them somewhere. They go everywhere: under the bed, under the guestroom bed, in the wardrobe, in the shoe cupboard, you name it, any nook and cranny is now stuffed with a box from Groupon. Somehow, despite the fact that my little darling usually roots through anything and everything, especially during hide and seek (or when she steals chocolate and goes to hide so she can eat it secretly without me noticing, except I am gifted, like most mothers, with eyes in the back of my head), she never actually twigs about all of those new boxes that have appeared. I just pray there isn't a fire, or we won't last five seconds.

The week before the school breaks up is Davina's first nativity at school. Now, deep down we all want our daughter to play the part of Mary. If your daughter is Mary, then you have earnt the right to be smug. Your child is the centre of attention and for once for something sweet as opposed to something embarrassing. Everyone will watch in awe at how sweet she will look and comment "Doesn't she handle the baby well?" If she doesn't make Mary, the next best part has to be an angel – there are usually three so there is a good chance she will get the part. But at age five, Davina lands the role of the back of the donkey. Proud beyond words, and guess whose children are the star roles? That's right, the organic baking bitch parade. Even the chav's children have good roles. The donkey's backside is what I am going to have to film to represent her first school nativity.

If it's not bad enough that my child is an arse, the fact that she insists on separating herself from the head makes it much worse. I mean, here is a perfect opportunity for her to remain hidden so no-one sees. Being disguised as a donkey's backside is supposed to have its perks. If someone asks, "What was Davina, I didn't see her?" I am supposed to be able to say, "Oh she was one of the angels, at the back." But no, not my little fruit pot, she decides to separate from the front end and parade herself around the stage in a one man show. And of course, who should just happen to be the front end of the donkey? Lionel! Lionel doesn't take too well to having his arse disappear, becomes upset and starts running around the stage shouting, "My bottom has gone." Well, as you can imagine, being gay parents with a child shouting he's lost his bottom is not the kind of attention you want to attract at the school play. And there it is, the shaking of the head from Mrs Crecher. That disappointed look, again. I look across to Carlton, who at this point is giving me the evil stare for having a child who won't keep her arse still and aligned!

The Christmas Tree

What's the phrase? I didn't know I had OCD until I allowed my child to decorate the tree! Now, Pete and I, after that one catastrophic fall-out on the lead up to Christmas, have discovered our roles in the Christmas tree set up.

Pete's Jobs:

1. Pay for the tree.
2. Strap said tree to roof of car.
3. Find stand in back of garage, bring into house and place tree in it.
4. (Probably should be 3) Remove spiders from tree stand.
5. Untangle Christmas tree lights from the mass ball I created last year.
6. Stand at other side of tree whilst I pass through fairy lights. Do not improvise, place them in the exact spot my arm directs.
7. Leave the room.

Jess's Jobs:

1. Pick the best tree.
2. Buy more Christmas decorations than needed.
3. Pour Baileys and put on Michael Buble at Christmas.

4. Wind fairy lights around the tree and arrange evenly, giving clear instructions to Pete.
5. Place baubles and beads on tree.
6. Stand back and marvel at my artistic flair.

Davina's Job:

1. Watch CBeebies.

Need I say more? There are just certain things in life I know I am best at and tree decorating is one of them. However, when the little angel turns five, she is aware that the decorations she made at school are not on the tree. Kids understand that decorating the tree is all part of the build up to Christmas and they want some of that action. And this is how we end up with two trees. The smaller version sits in the dining room, in the corner, and I would end it there but you know as well as I do that once she's gone to bed, it will be re-arranged.

Christmas Eve

Now if you thought the OCD only stretched to the Christmas tree... wrong. There is just something about Christmas Eve that means my child has to replicate everything I did on Christmas Eve when I was a child. It has to be a carrot for Rudolf – there is no way he can have an apple just because Davina doesn't like carrots – and Santa always has a brandy and a mince pie – offering an alcohol free beer and a weight watchers ginger bread slice ain't gonna wash. I don't care what they teach you. Christmas Eve is magical. The Christmas Police aren't on duty that night and, let's face it, it's actually the reindeer flying that sleigh tonight so Santa can get shitfaced. I insist that she goes to bed extra early and for once there are no arguments. I read her *The Night Before Christmas*, what else would I read? I tuck her in, kiss her cheek and make the usual threat: "If you don't go to sleep, Santa won't come." It's a little cruel, really, sending your little one to sleep with such a daunting thought, but it's for their own good – if they were to catch us being Santa when only aged five, the damage would be irreparable and I can guarantee she would tell everyone in her class that Santa isn't real. I would be lynched in the playground by the other parents. I head downstairs. I usually wait a good half hour before I go out with the bag of white flour and start making foot prints on the path. This is then followed by jingling some bells just under her window, in case she is still up. Of course, one of us needs to be inside just in case she decides to come down and catches us out, but she doesn't, not tonight.

Then starts the wrapping marathon. I suddenly feel like I am racing against the clock. *Did I really buy this much shit?* I ask myself. The disapproval is written all over Pete's face but he daren't say anything. No-one wants to fall out on Christmas Eve. I am surrounded by a mountain of presents and begin to wonder if I've time to wrap all of them. What will help, of course, is a glass of wine. After Pete's been instructed to open a bottle, he sits back and stokes the fire, because that's what he is good at, and I start the wrapathon.

For some reason, despite knowing we are going to be up at the crack of dawn, that my feet literally aren't going to touch the ground, save for present opening, I decide that tonight would be a good night for two bottles of wine and a Baileys. It is Christmas, after all. By the end of the evening, I've no bottom lip left due to deciding to bite off the cellotape as opposed to cutting it off, and I'm feeling a little frisky. Suddenly, the thought of a man I don't know with a full sack heading into our house turns me on. I decide tonight is the night when I will try on that outfit Pete bought me last Christmas, the one with the white stockings. After doing my slutty walk, I burst into a song of *Santa Baby*. Pete, being Pete, well, any male really, is obviously up for it. And so begins a good one hour shagathon. One hour, I hear you say. Don't worry, your other half isn't inferior, it's just that I like to build up the moment. Having had those two bottles of wine, I am suddenly like a kid at a theme park. I want to try every ride. I'm like the Duracell bunny on steroids. The actual deed itself only takes about five minutes; once I pass out, it doesn't take Pete long to get where he needs to be. As for me, no water, fast asleep in an all in one see through white body with matching stockings. I wake at some point around 02.30ish. It seems like I've been asleep for hours but I remember it was 12.15 when I last looked at the clock. My tongue is attached to the roof of my mouth and my head has its own heart beat – again. I grab a plastic cup from Davina's toy room and fill it with lukewarm water from the bathroom tap, then another and another. After scurrying through the medicine cabinet for paracetamol, I opt for Sinutab since it's the only thing I can find. I figure it's head related so must work to remove the beat, and head back to bed. And there I lie, for the next two and a half hours. Everything I can possibly imagine runs through my head. I think about all sorts. It starts with Christmas morning. *Must remember to put the oven on before we open the presents to get it warmed up, mustn't forget to cook the non-meat versions of stuffing I bought.* It then moves to, *what will we watch Boxing Day, which chocolates shall I gorge today?* It then moves to much greater things, like how lucky we are, how we indulge so much when so many have so little. *What if that happened to us, what if we lost everything, what if we were born into a different country, what if we weren't Davina's parents or God forbid she was stolen from us?* And that's how the next two and half hours pass. Finally, at around five a.m. I fall asleep. I am dead to the world until a great thundering sound comes barging through our room.

"Mummy, Daddy, he hasn't been, he hasn't been," sobs a distraught five year old.

Crap, we forgot her stocking. (When you forget the tooth fairy, there is a number of excuses. "It was the Tooth Fairy's Christmas Party, it was Tooth Fairies Bank Holiday, the Queen Tooth Fairies Jubilee. Sadly, none of these excuses work on the evening when Santa actually works!). Although she's only five, she knows the time, she knows when it's seven a.m. and when it's eight a.m.

Seven a.m. during the week means half a smile from Mummy when I wake her up, eight a.m. on a weekend means a bigger smile from Mummy. 05.30 a.m. and no Santa means trouble.

"I've been bad."

I elbow Pete and whisper through Davina's sobs to go fill up her stocking, which must still be hanging over the fireplace. The pile of small presents all ready for the stocking must still be at the bottom of the stairs. Bless Pete, he's so much better in a crisis than I am for he grabs those presents, stuffs them in that stocking and re-emerges, suggesting to Davina that she forgot to look under her bed. (Thank goodness we have two staircases). Davina, not convinced at all, staggers back to her room as though her soul has been removed from her body. However, when she then sees that stocking brimming with presents, that frown is soon turned upside down. Great, now we can all go back to sleep – yeah, right – like chuff we can!

And so it begins, Christmas morning. The excitement, the fun, the look on their tiny faces. This is what it's about. This is actually why we had kids in the first place, to tell them a big fat lie, build up their hopes and dreams and then let it all come crashing down when they are about ten-ish. But it's so worth it.

Our Christmas morning always starts with the stocking in bed and coffee, lots of coffee. Pete and I stopped doing stockings for one another once Davina arrived. Before Davina, Pete used to do the most amazing stocking for me, there would be a bottle of Coco Channel, leather gloves, underwear (the type you can actually fit your arse in and it looks good), chocolates, a CD, tickets for a pop concert, and this was just the start. I always felt really bad – whilst I was opening my perfume, Pete would be unwrapping a pair of Marks & Spencers socks and a box of Toffifee. Bless him, one year, whilst I was unwrapping my Mulberry purse, he was unwrapping his wellie warmers. I've never known anyone talk about wellie warmers so enthusiastically before, but that's just Pete. He loves the little things in life.

Pete and I wait until Davina has gone to bed now to open our presents. The budget has significantly reduced but I don't mind: after all, I'm not earning a salary anymore. I won't say I'm not working because Davina is a full time job! You can always tell when cash is tight as instead of the La Perla underwear, it's now a sensible pack of three underwear from Accessories, practical and big enough to cover my arse. Gone are the days of the beaded G-string.

So back to Christmas morning. Davina becomes like a child possessed. It no longer matters what is in the packages, it's just about opening them all, as fast as humanly possible. I'm trying to take note of who bought what, but this moves from full names and doodles to initials and a quick sketch. Within ten minutes, I can no longer see carpet, just a flood of Christmas wrappings with mounting toys. *Ah well, that's what it's all about*, I tell myself, knowing fine well that if I had ever behaved like this on Christmas day I would have got a clip around the ear. So, it's 6.45 a.m. The presents are opened, what next? Pete, once again, is going through his plethora of batteries, the screwdriver is out and he means business!

As I enter the kitchen to commence the cookathon, I hear a loud screeching sound. I run into the lounge and see Davina shaking, and I mean literally shaking, the Real Life Baby Annabel, who is crying. "Shut up, shut up, you stupid baby," comes out the mouth of my child. *She's just tired*, I tell myself. After Pete finishes putting in the triple As on the final toy, she's bored. She sits looking around as though she is sat amongst a giant pile of shit. She picks up toys, looks at them and throws them down in utter disgust. The ungrateful little sh...

"Mummy, I been bad."

"Pardon, darling?"

"I been bad, Santa not bring me a My Little Pony bed."

"But, darling, I don't remember seeing the My Little Pony bed on your list."

"I told him, Mummy, I told him at the garden centre. Remember, Mummy, the Santa who I said wasn't Santa but you said it was, he had just had a busy morning?"

"Well, sweet, Santa cannot remember everything and I think you did very well. I mean, look, you've the Sullivan Family Mansion and yacht."

"But I didn't ask for that, Mummy, and you won't let me move anything. I been bad, Mummy. Sorrreee, Santa." She says this to the Santa cam. Oh God, I spent £650.00 and she's not happy. I suck at this. How come my parents made Christmas Day so magical and special, and I didn't get half the stuff she has? A soap on a rope, apple and an orange stuffed in my stocking was the best thing on earth. What happened? How did I get it so wrong? Ungrateful little... Turkey, it's time to put the turkey in. Bollocks, I've been sat pondering for the past half an hour, outlaws are arriving in approximately ninety minutes. Okay, I can do this. Now this is the ultimate test for my mother-in-law. Since I refuse to go to theirs for Christmas dinner and insist they come to us (actually, I don't insist and would prefer it if they would just go on a very long vacation over the Christmas period), she will test me to see if I can produce something edible and warm – not just a warm plate, the entire contents on it need to be warm too. Despite how close to perfection my Yorkshires raise, or how there are no lumps in the gravy, she will not be able to resist finding some way in which to prove her culinary skills are better. For example, "Oh, Roger, do you remember that time I stuffed an ostrich with a penguin, in a swan, stuffed with duck and monkey testicles, it was soooo tender." Okay, perhaps not quite what happened, but that's what it sounded like to me. It's usually:

"Is the turkey from the supermarket?"

"Yes, Aldi had a great offer on."

"Ahh I thought so. You know, our local butcher, Clive, does the best free range Norfolk Black Turkeys. The meat is so moist, isn't it Roger?"

Of course, Roger doesn't give a shit, so long as he is stuffing his face and drinking most of our expensive Malbec, he's quite happy but he knows when to agree at the appropriate time and a simple "yes, dear" is enough to satisfy her and keep her smiling. I recall one year, I actually made homemade mince pies, with proper homemade pastry and everything. Okay, so I bought the mincemeat, but everything else I did myself. I grated lemon zest, made and rolled out the pastry, and even stuffed each little parcel with a whole clementine segment, and I have to say, they were the dogs dangly bits. When offering them out to Roger, he initially withdrew, telling me how Janet grates orange zest into hers but when I told him there was actually a whole clementine segment in there, he almost looked impressed. Of course, he wasn't allowed to enjoy it as she was glaring at him the entire time. There was no spoken word, but I could see the look in her eyes: "You dare say they are better than mine and you will be eating baked beans for the next year." Roger, bless his soul, simply ate the one, although I know deep down he would have eaten the whole bloody lot, so good they were!

Now, since it's Christmas morning and the hangover is slowly wearing off and I've just finished scrambled eggs and smoked salmon, now seems a really good time to open the fizz. Pete and I always buy a case of the champagne we had on our wedding day. Since Christmas Day fizz used to be our thing before Davina, it was our special treat to ourselves and whilst we have cut back on the gifts, there is no way we are cutting back on the Christmas Day booze. In the good old days, the before D days, we would happily polish off four bottles in the blink of an eye. I'd be peeling the sprouts, put Nat King Cole Christmas Special on whilst Pete took care of the turkey.

I never remembered how the dinner actually tasted because I was always so pissed. By about four p.m., we were wasted. We would have our traditional Christmas Day shag in the converted attic (I'm not sure what it was about the attic but it just felt right on Christmas Day), followed by a Cuban cigar. After that, we would fall asleep then wake around ten and watch the latest Bond film, stuffing leftover turkey, roast potatoes and stuffing. Aahh, the good old days. Now, I drink half a bottle of fizz in the morning and I'm as high as a kite. I cannot drink any more or else I will be asleep on the sofa, and Pete has warned me that if I miss Christmas again, he will pour the bloody stuff down the sink!

After dinner has been served and devoured, and Davina has told every crappy joke from the crackers at least four times, we all sit down in the lounge and feel absolutely bloody knackered. Everything is an effort at this point. Michael McIntyre can be on the telly and it's still too much of an effort to laugh at his jokes. I swear my ears are leaking roasted parsnips and pigs in blankets. For some reason, this one day of the year is the day I choose to pile as much as will fit on my plate as possible, and I eat the whole goddamn lot. Not only that – despite being full to bursting, I then eat my way through a giant-sized portion of Christmas pudding, which, truth be told, I don't actually like, but it's Christmas and it's not Christmas unless you have a flaming Christmas pudding. Why? Why do we do it to ourselves? It's not like we've never had a Sunday dinner before. We are Yorkshire folk, we have one every bloody Sunday and never eat that much!

It's usually around this time, when we are stuffed and knackered, that the outlaws feel now is a good time to hand out their presents. I don't know why they make us wait. Is it better that way? Does she think that dragging it out actually makes the gift better? If she does, she needs to wait about ten fucking years, and even then it will still suck. My favourites so far have been the texting gloves, gloves you can text in. I feel I have to explain because that's how she explained it to me. This and *How to Eat Healthy in Old Age* were particular favourites of mine. I've often wondered if Pete's mother actually likes me. I tell myself she does because she always hugs me really tightly and tells me how lucky Pete is to have a wife who fulfills his life. At least, I think she says fulfills...

Of course, then there is my family. We never see each other on Christmas Day and we are all quite happy with that. The truth is, if you stick us all in room, we argue. We aren't your aggressive types, but we are all straight talking loud mouths. It only takes one comment about how I baste my bird and the whole bloody room can erupt. My mother says I'm sensitive but to me it's not sensitivity, I just get annoyed when she's over my shoulder doing a run by run commentary on how to baste a turkey. I find with my own family I cannot contain the annoyance and I blow, it's the easiest way and the only way to get them to listen. The problem is, once one blows, the rest follow. Poor Pete has ended up trying to mediate between my family and I on a few occasions at a family gathering. He looked genuinely hurt when my Grandma told him to go and fuck himself. So, instead of the potential for an explosive Christmas Day, we usually gather a few days after Christmas. That way, we've usually eaten and drunk so much we don't actually give a shit anymore. A bout of food poisoning would be welcome at this point to stop us eating. However, the other problem with my family is we all like a drink. Usually the day before my family arrives, Pete starts hiding all our best wine and liquor. He puts them in places I don't know exist, as he knows that if I get my hands on his unique blend of Scotch Whisky I will be using it as a cocktail known as the Jessiculator. On most family gatherings like this, I usually find Pete sitting in a corner, pretending to be invisible. I swear he's counting one one thousand, two one thousand, just to help it pass. Although, to be fair, the first Christmas family gathering we had with my family resulted in my mum and Pete with tea towels around their head and blow up guitars, singing to Europe. He puked up all night having drunk too much Fuckedtail (another unique blend).

Boxing Day is probably the best part of Christmas. I stay in my pyjamas all day, eat leftover turkey and cranberry sandwiches, drink copious amounts of red wine and stuff myself silly with chocolate whilst watching *Wizard of Oz*, *Sinbad*, *Return to Witch Mountain* and *Love Actually*. That is, of course, in between dealing with a whining child who continually asks why it can't be Christmas every day.

Chapter Six
Another Year

I hate New Year. I hate the whole charade of making promises you have no intention of keeping. It marks the end of Christmas. You are about to head into four months of dreary, cold, miserable, life-sucking weather. Each New Year always starts the same: I will need to lose at least a stone from everything I've eaten and drunk at Christmas. I circle our next holiday on the calendar and note it's July, ffs. There really is nothing to look forward to in January and on the 1st of January my moping starts. Pete really pisses me off with his cheery disposition. He always starts every year with the same mantra: "I'm going to kick this year's arse and make it right for me." Whoopie doos! He actually wakes up happy on News Year Day, which really fucks me off. He always shaves off the beard he has grown over Christmas. It's some kind of ritual he does every year, like he's shedding and removing any trace of the previous year. And another thing that really pisses me off is that despite the fact he ate more than me over Christmas (didn't drink as much as me) he has barely put on any weight. In fact, one year I swear he lost some. I once bought him a pair of jeans a size too small, just to make him think he had piled on the pounds, but they bloody fit him. It's usually this time of year when I want to grab Pete's head and smash it against the wall. Call it hormones, depression, whatever you like, but I ain't happy and for some reason, this year feels particularly bad. Even more of a reason to not be happy this year is that now that Davina has started school, there really is no excuse why I can't start looking for some part-time work. I can't go back to what I used to do, marketing manager for a large chocolate factory. They don't want part time staff and the hours can be really unsociable, so what am I supposed to do? As if he was enjoying my pain, Pete came back from our local village shop the other day informing me that there is a part time job going there, three days a week. My lack of poker face said it all, really. When I added that I was aware, and that in addition they want you to work every other weekend, which would mean he would need to care for Davina on his own whilst I was at work, he soon retreated.

It's around mid-January when I hit the sales. I cannot bear it any earlier, all those women who start a fight with you if you happen to walk past their man are in the shops, particularly one brand of shop which has such massive reductions that people queue from like four a.m – I mean, get a life! Socks are socks, the fact they now cost 50p doesn't change the fact they are socks. Since Davina turned five, I thought she might have turned that corner where she actually starts to enjoy shopping – wrong. The only thing she likes to do is go into the Body Shop, sniff the bubble bath and mix up the lipsticks so the poor lady who thinks she is buying pink blush will actually be wearing fuck me red. The fact the outlet actually has a huge play area to reward a good shopping trip would probably entice most children to grin and bear it. But not Davina. That's not enough, she wants to know what there is there, who will be there, how long she can play there; the incessant chatter doesn't allow me to shop because I can no longer focus. Even when I manage to tune out Davina's noise, there is always that mother who feels the need to explain very loudly every darn thing she is thinking and her child is doing. "What, Conroy, you want to buy those pyjamas? But you've got ten pairs of Spiderman pyjamas." Why does she feel the need to announce this to everyone? Is it that she is so insecure in her parenting that she has to ensure everyone supports her decision making? Or is to do with Conroy, who wants to buy so many pjyamas so he can stuff them in his ears and drown out the sound of his mother? It's these women who never lose the baby weight. They won't even try. It's their brandishing of motherhood. "I am fat but I had a baby, he is eighteen now but I had a baby and therefore I deserve to stay this fat." Of course, they are the ones whose husbands are on the dating websites each night, pretending they are thirty somethings with a six pack.

As January goes by, Pete becomes jollier and I become more miserable. He's been advised he is line for the next promotion. He will no longer manage a team of ten IT consultants, but potentially will be managing all the units across the country. Of course, this is great news – it's more money and means he will be working away a lot more. Right now, that really doesn't bother me. At least I won't have to put up with him grinding his teeth every night and doing that jaw wobble thing. It also takes a bit of pressure off from a financial point of view and means it's not so urgent that I look for a job. Great, but now what do I moan about? As the weeks drag on, it's all about Pete: he's out for dinners, corporate entertaining. He has started looking at brochures for his new car. He no longer seems impressed with my homemade falafel tart or spiced roasted squash stew. He doesn't even notice when I have my hair coloured red. It's all me, me, me. All I get now when I talk about what I have been doing is a "Hmm, hmm, ooohh, right." To be fair, I am not really sure what else there is to say to, "I took Davina to school, spoke to Carlton, went to body pump, came home, showered, tidied up, picked up Davina, made tea." Still, he could at least try to sound interested.

It's towards the end of January when I seriously start getting worried about myself. The fact that I woke up this morning with a thrill because it's green bin day confirmed just how very dull my life has become. Just as I start to think my wallowing in self-pity could actually be a medical problem i.e. under or over active thyroid, I get a ping from Faye on messenger:

"Aye up, chick sticks, so I've spoken to Lou and we've agreed on Prague for Leigh's hen do. I've worked on prices and it all fits within the budget and the dates you gave. 20th March, two nights, flight and accommodation, £400. Just need numbers to confirm and we are booking. I know you are in, right?"

Humph, I say to myself, humph that they didn't consult me before choosing the venue, bloody Prague. It will be freezing in March. If they had thought to consult me, I would have suggested somewhere warm and sunny, like Tenerife, not bloody Prague. Well, I will just have to check my very busy diary and get back to them. I can't check it now because I'm busy, doing stuff that needs to be done, so they can just wait and sweat for a bit!

After twenty minutes of prime sulking, I message back. "In! Details for booking, please." A ping straight back has flight company and sort code and bank account for Faye, who will secure the accommodation. Within another twenty minutes it's done. I'm booked. Something unexpected then happens, a smile creeps across my face. Two nights away with the girls. Okay, so they didn't discuss the venue with me, but does it really matter? Two nights of freedom, no child, no Pete, no housework, no gym. Finally, something to look forward to.

When Pete gets home, I'm a little upbeat and he notices. "Hey, you look great," he says as he walks through the door. Obviously the smile is an improvement. I've cooked another of his favourite meals, crusted lamb chops with mint and puree peas and a good helping of roast potatoes. The look on his face says at all: "I'm getting laid tonight." Pah! You fool. As I serve him the remaining lamb chops and drizzle over the remaining sauce, I decide now is a good time to remind him of the hen weekend. Like me, he has no poker face either.

"I don't remember you telling me about that." I stare. "I mean, I remember you telling me that one was going to be organised, but you never confirmed the date." I still stare, a little harder this time. He is floundering.

"I told you the dates. In fact, you gave me the dates."

"But, but, but," is all he can muster.

"Check your IPhone 6 diary, sweetie, I'm sure it's in there."

He grabs for the phone, not believing a word I am telling him, and there it is. The look on his face says it all. D & D over the two days commencing 20th March. He is defeated and I am smug.

"But that's a Friday, and what with the promotion…" I cannot hear anything because the water is running as I rinse off the dishes. It's at this point the penny drops, he's worked it out: the smile, the nice meal – he's not getting sex, I am going away, and not just away, away with the girls. As I turn towards him, he opens his mouth to speak but then he decides against it. My look has said it all. It's that "don't fuck with me" look. He knows it well and knows if he pushes it, there will be outright war. There is no point negotiating this. He should know deep down that I've spoken to his mother and she is ready and armed for her granddaughter and dutiful son, despite her comments of, "Oh, I could never leave Peter."

Pete is sulking – he pretends he isn't but it's so there.

"So, where are you going?" he eventually asks.

"Prague."

This pleases him. It's cold and he knows I have an aversion to cold. Our heating bill isn't over £300 per month because I'm growing weed, although that could be a career move. Somehow, the mention of Prague pleases him. He knows I won't be scantily clad and looking my best (having a tan always makes you look your best). Suddenly, he is actually quite excited for me.

"Prague is supposed to be lovely, a continental European version of York, you'll have a great time."

I nod and smile. *Oh yes, I will*, I say to myself, with a slightly evil, sinister giggle. I decide I'm going to find my old self in Prague.

Chapter Seven
Prague Part One

I've worked my arse off, and I mean literally off; there is not a pound of flesh on that bony joint. Of course, it involved a lot of hard work. I briefed Jade about the hen weekend and she has literally beaten my arse into a piece of stone. My face has some shape again, there is a definite distinction between my chin and neck and I look like my old self again. In fact, I must been looking good right now because the fit bitch brigade even invite me for a peppermint tea with them after body pump, which of course I accept without hesitation. It's only when the talk turns to Oscar's acceptance to Cambridge at age seven and Jasper's starring role in Jesus Christ Superstar, York version, that I decide I have nothing in common with these people.

Now, it's mandatory amongst my friends that when there is a hen do we have to get dressed up. For some reason, being able to wear 'normal' clothing and go out and enjoy yourself is no longer acceptable. Don't get me wrong, it's not tacky, there are no banners, veils or condoms, or builders outfits for that matter – it's slightly more tasteful. As Leigh has a nickname of 'Princess' it seemed entirely appropriate for us all to dress up as the cast of Cinderella. It sounds fanciful but it's pretty difficult to pull this look off. Luckily for me, I just happen to have stashed in the back of my wardrobe a Marie Antoinette costume. When I inform Faye of this, she insists we be the ugly sisters. (Of course, we make sure we look our very best). Princess Leigh is, of course, Cinderella, and we have a suitable Cinderella costume for her, pre ball. Then there is the prince, and Lou is quite happy to dress up as a handsome prince. So that leaves the mice and the Fairy Godmother. Well, those roles can go out on the email for some of Leigh's other friends to select. I'm sorted.

I'm at the airport. Faye and I got a lift to the airport from Pete and Davina. He wants to be with me for every last second before I leave. I'm certain it's not because he doesn't want me to go, but because he doesn't want to be in charge of the monster on his own. I kiss them both goodbye and watch as the car drives out of sight.

Prosecco, is the first thing that crosses my mind. After check in and security, we find ourselves in the bar. Now I can really relax. Before I know it, a second bottle is opened and it's at this point that Leigh and Lou arrive, closely followed by some giggling girls and a chubby man, no, woman, following closely behind.

Introductions are given and I look around at my comrades for this weekend's shenanigans. The three mice are all pretty much the same: young, slim, blonde and eager as chuff. They laugh at everything and clearly think the sun shines out of Leigh's arse. I think I can tolerate them. As for the he/she/me bird, she is a different ball game. At first glance she looks very hostile, until I realise

– she is just really really out of place. Leigh grabs her and pulls her in. "So, this is my lover, Bridget." *Ah, she's gay.* Well, of course she is gay, no heterosexual girl wears that. A Leeds United Football Shirt is so last... erm, never.

I'm boarding the plane. I feel as light as a feather. I hate flying but, somehow, right now I actually feel like I could fly. I love prosecco! We board the Ryanair, no frills, aircraft. Of course, being the last call, as we board everyone is glaring. We are those people you swear you will never be. There should never be a need to make a final call to get passengers on the plane. You are leaving the shitty stormy weather of the UK behind to hot, sweaty sun. You should always be checking the board. The minute your gate number appears, you run to that plane and get on it so you can leave this cold, wet, dreary country. It's always the same people who turn up last on the plane, the ones that smoke and have ten bags of duty free consisting of cigarettes and alcohol. Except today, of course, we are the drunken ladies, late because we forgot to check the screen.

The good thing about being a group of girls/women is that when we board the plane, the only glaring looks are from the women, and that's nice. I like that. I always want to be that woman that pisses off another woman by my mere presence. If she didn't give a shit, what is the point? The reality is, as you get older, you just want the attention from other women. If they looked pissed off, you know you are doing something right.

Since we are at the last call, our seats are limited and we are spread out like a tarts knickers. Faye is at least four rows behind, but that's not necessarily a bad thing. The two of us together on a three and a half hour flight is not good. There would be singing, roaring and several profanities. I sit next to a loving couple. Turns out they are taking their first mini break together, how sweet. After lecturing them about contraception – and not for warnings of an STD but, even worse, a child – they seem less interested in talking to me. Behind me are the giddy kippers, the mice for Cinderella's carriage. I try them out for about fifteen minutes whilst waiting for the drinks trolley. A void in my life has been fulfilled. I know exactly where Bobby Brown's misty look sits on your lids and the entire life story of Justin Bieber (I have not been Biebered, only in *Apocalypse Now* could that ever happen).

I recline in my chair. I never recline normally but the skinny bitches behind me won't notice a thing. That is, until I feel a wet patch on the back of my neck. As I reach to check, bam, there's another. It's like a drip. *Fuck me, the plane is underwater.* Drip. There it is again. I check to see if we underwater, phew, I can see a cloud shaped like a dolphin. Drip. Again, this time followed by a snort. *Haha, you bitch.* I turn around and see Faye in hysterical laughter four rows behind. I always told her that gap in her front teeth was good for lots of things. She never wakes up tasting yesterday's roast chicken. She's obviously been working on her range and four seats back is pretty good going. I am proud. I look around to see if I can share it with anyone – alas, I am on my own, so I chuckle to myself. When the drinks trolley arrives, I order four bottles of prosecco (they are only small), two for me and two for Faye. As the hostess delivers the two bottles to Faye, a floating kiss smacks my cheek. Aah, I love her.

As the plane lands I am totally shitfaced. Trying to walk off the plane is like I am walking on the moon. At the exit I am greeted by the air hostess ladies and their she bitch. The she bitch is rather taken with me. She/him (shim) compliments me on my outfit and bangs on the door. Out arrives shim's civil partner, Derek, the Captain. I praise shim on a great cockpit pull and vacate the aircraft.

Our group rekindles somewhere around passport control. All are accounted for and present. Some are slightly more inebriated than others. Faye and I, for instance, decide that doing the Macarena through passport control might be really entertaining for what looks like a really dull job, but apparently not. Being approached by two male guards with very large guns gives us a clear message that this kind of behaviour is unacceptable. I suddenly miss Pete. He would protect me from these foreigners. At least I think he would…

Somehow, we make it through security and into the luggage waiting area. Now, if you are like me, this has to be the worst part of your holiday. It's the same fear you used to get when in the girls' gym changing room, being selected for a team. Will you be chosen? *Please don't let me be last.* I was never last, thankfully, second to last is not last. Waiting for your luggage is the same. Will it turn up? Everyone else's luggage is riding past but not mine. Who the fuck buys a luminous pink suitcase with tiger paw prints on the front? When have you ever been into Samsonite and they have had that on display? It's always black or burnt grey. As one of the three mice step forward to retrieve the pink paw printed suitcase, all clicks into place. By some miracle, my luggage arrives. I marvel at myself for recognising it, although I think it has been past a few times. Davina's hair bobble is tied around the handles. I miss Pete again. We are a full set and match, until Faye realises she has left her Save The Queen leather jacket on the plane. And this is why we should have paid a premium for allocated seating! She is, of course, at this point in a heap on the floor in the luggage hall. Having clocked the men with big guns looking at us, with the scene that is being created before me, I decide action needs to be taken. I head back towards the aircraft. I don't know if you have ever tried this, before but not even Lara Croft could get through. There is no reversing. Not even a Trojan Horse would fool these fellows, let alone my best swagger. But this won't do, I cannot have my bestie in such bother at this stage in the hen weekend. I eventually find a rep, one that looks gay and is slightly bored. After discussing our predicament, it is clear he is bored of assigning coaches and sets about retrieving the leather jacket. Thirty minutes later, and who should come swaggering down the luggage hall? None other than Mr Rep himself. He has the leather jacket draped over his left shoulder and swans down the hall like it's a catwalk. As he takes the jacket off his shoulder, he launches it into the air. Faye tries to catch it but it lands in a heap on the floor next to her. We both hug him. Faye goes for a kiss but he waggles his finger at her, a clear no.

Somehow, I find myself in a pre-booked car, heading away from the airport and into the lights of the City of Prague. It's at this point I enjoy the fact other people take control. However, the missing jacket incident has sobered me up a little. I can focus again and it actually looks really pretty. There is something here, it's not York, the buildings look slightly mythical, and it's a bit like I've just stepped into a Disney movie, except instead of Minnie Mouse, Jessica Rabbit has just landed, possibly with fangs. We arrive at our hotel. I can't help but laugh rather loudly at the reception boy, who genuinely looks like something from Bram Stoker's *Dracula*. I say reception, it's a desk at the base of the staircase. There is no lift, which I am pleased about since that's a clear sign there will be no babies or old people here. This is perhaps where the Phantom Raspberry Blower possibly retired to. We are given the keys to the floor apartment. The staircase is a challenge, but Faye and I manage to make it to the top unscathed.

One we get into the pad, we sort out our beds. Faye and I have bagged ourselves two single beds just opposite the toilet. There was no need for discussion about this, we saw the room and its location to the toilet and our arses were on those beds faster than a Scotsman on the way to a free bar. We have both, after all, had children, and therefore our bladders are not quite the same. I see a tap drip and I need a piss. Within the quickest time ever in the history of getting ready for a night out, I am ready and in the lounge. It took all of about ten minutes. The fact there is no booze in the pad has nothing to do with it. After five minutes of waiting, I suggest to Faye that perhaps we should wait in the bar next to the hotel until everyone is ready. It's clear the giddy kippers are going to take an awful lot longer than I am prepared to wait.

When we are all gathered in the bar, to be honest it's a bit of an anticlimax. We are here, most of us are strangers to one another. This fact didn't bother me when we were in the airport, but now I am sober again, I realise that polite chit chat is actually quite boring. I am here, sat in the bar, having a dull conversation about nothing in particular – it's kinda like, now what? It sounds so obvious, but a game of truth or dare gets started in an effort to bond us. Of course, it was Faye's idea. The opening question from one of the giddy kippers is "Have you had two men at once?"

A nonchalant, "Yes" comes from Faye's mouth.

All is quiet. I look at Faye. "Uni," she whispers, "football team." Ah, well that explains it then. I'm a little surprised I didn't know this before. And to think I thought I was a rebel at uni, perhaps not so much.

It moves to the gay question. Bridget has perked up. It's Princess's turn. "Have you ever snogged a girl?" Of course, Bridget is excluded. Faye shuffles. In fact, Faye suggests more drinks. Is this because my glass is empty? No, it's still half full. Hmm. The question moves around the table.

I bide my time and wait until Faye gets back to the table. "Have you ever snogged a girl?" I ask Faye. She doesn't answer. She sips her drink and requests the next question. Meanwhile, I find her hand on my knee. I feel a shiver down my spine. Happy days?

We leave the bar and head somewhere, who knows where, but we are moving away from the hotel. Thankfully, the next bar has a dance floor, and one thing most women have in common is the appreciation of a dance floor. Normally, I am one with the dance floor, but somehow, this time, amongst partial strangers, I don't want to strut just yet. I am clearly still sober and am now starting to think I might get an early night and enjoy a lie in. Of course, then Faye straddles across and whips out her pretend fishing rod to reel me in. Somehow, the need for an early night disappears and the need for a shot suddenly is upon me. Forty five Euros later, Faye and I are having our own little party on the dance floor. Of course, by now, we are bored here. We have straddled every object and flirted with the DJ, now it's time to leave. When we suggest we leave, the rest of the group wimp out. There are excuses coming at us left, right and centre. Even the bride-to-be wants to head off. WTF. I look at Faye and she looks at me – there are no words said but we are both thinking the same thing: *There is no fucking way I am going back now.* As the group disperses, there is just Faye and I and someone called Rhonda. I'm not even sure if she part of our group but she looks like she might be so we allow her to remain. So, where now? It's at this point in the evening, once the crowd of girlies around us has dispensed, that the other sex see the protective shield has been breached. They can now penetrate (in their dreams), the force field. Of course, we are up for any attention from the opposite sex, any male who hasn't seen that your tits now look like spaniels ears, or the fact you can braid your pubic hair into a French plait, is well received. I need the confidence boost. It's nice to pretend the chicken fillets stuffed in my bra really are my actual boobs. The guys we are talking to want to take us to a bar where there is a proper DJ. We agree, but as we leave the bar, those familiar warning sirens are starting to sound. *I don't know them, what do they want, we are clearly a bit tipsy, what are their intentions?* Before I say a word, Faye is already in there. "So, what do you do?"

"We run a cereal factory, producing cereal."

"Cereal killers," I whisper to Faye.

She's laughing, but then stops and gives me that look. I know that look because I've seen that look before, it's the look of 'I've just had a little wee'. God love motherhood. With my sensible head on, just in case they really are serial killers, I insist they walk a good ten feet in front of us. That way, we will be safe. I marvel at myself for being the responsible one. Turns out, the cereal killers were right; they take us to an awesome bar. It's like giant greenhouse. It's ultra-trendy – there is exposed brickwork on the walls, a glass staircase and a glass bar. Then there are giant pots of tropical plants all around. The DJ is on a glass balcony, directly above what looks like a glass dance floor. Now we are talking. The cereal killers buy us some cocktails but, after downing them, we find an appropriate moment for the toilet run and hit the dance floor. Rhonda is still with us – she doesn't say much but seems happy to be in our company. My groove is on. I'm so pleased I lost those extra pounds. I feel magical being on this dance floor, in a city I've never been to before, with my best friend. I am beginning to feel emotional. I need a hug. I throw my arms around Faye.

"I love you," I slur.

"I love you too," she slurs back.

It's at this point my inner lesbian emerges and I plant a kiss on Faye's lips. Just a 'you're my best friend, I love you' sort of kiss. Okay, so Faye may have stuck her tongue in, but she was just messing. Rhonda then turns up with a tray full of shots and the rest of the night passes blissfully by.

At some point, I'm not sure of the exact time, we leave the bar. We step outside and there is already five inches of snow on the ground. Within seconds of opening the door, I slip, taking Faye and Rhonda with me. Our legs are in the air and our arses are laid on the snowy ground. Heels in this weather is a massive no-no. After laughing hysterically, I try to get up and help them up, except that blasted ice and down I go again. It's funnier this time because now we have given in and are doing snow angels. However, that warning bell rings again. *It's time to go home now.* After scraping myself up, latching up against the lamppost, I slide my way across to a taxi. Rhonda and Faye are supporting one another, taking around one step forward and three back. I manage to get us a taxi and, somehow, the taxi driver and I manage to escort Faye and Rhonda into the car. We are sat in the back. The taxi driver asks where we are going and it's at this point I release I have no fucking clue.

"Erm, a hotel, the one next to the bar, close to here." The language is clearly a barrier. I look to Faye. "Faye," (who has stayed here before), where are we staying?"

She responds, "Fokdgil giflild, finnme."

"Faye, where are we staying?"

"Hmm, yeah, yeah, yeah."

Okay, don't panic. "Rhonda, Rhonda, where are we staying?"

"Who's Rhonda?"

Fuck! Okay, don't panic. It's snowing, we are somewhere in Eastern Europe, staying in a hotel which you have absolutely no idea what it is called. *Don't panic*, I tell myself, but that's not really working. What to do, what to do? After trying to describe the reception and bellboy, I realise I'm getting nowhere. Then I remember the kitty, a small Hello Kitty purse stuffed with hundreds of pounds which everyone paid into earlier for the weekend's drinks. Well, this is a matter of life and death, I am sure they will understand. "Take us to your finest hotel," I say, pleased that once again I am being the sensible one.

"The Four Seasons," is the response. I nod. That will do, I don't think I could actually think of a finer hotel. We are, after all, in Eastern Europe, we cannot afford to stay in some dodgy 'slit your neck whilst you are sleeping' kind of hotel.

We arrive at the Four Seasons. Now, this is the part where deep down I feel like this is where I truly belong. But that's deep down. Outwardly, I look like I belong back on the floor, just outside the bar we just left.

Unsurprisingly, the Four Seasons reception is quiet at 02.00 a.m. and for this I am grateful. There will be no need for a scene, we can get a room and sleep off the best of what is probably going to be an almighty hangover in goose down bedding and drink bottled spring water from a waterfall from heaven.

"One double room," I say, using my best soberish voice. Rhonda can sleep on the floor.

The man behind the reception desk looks from me to the other two, who are staggering either side of me, desperately trying to stand straight. He taps into the computer. "That will be two hundred and eight five Euros" he says.

"What, but half the night has gone, we will have to check out at eleven a.m? Can't you do a reduced rate?"

"That is the reduced rate."

"Oh."

I empty the entire contents of the kitty onto the reception counter and to my delight there is 400.00 Euros in it. I slide over the cash.

"And your ID?" he asks.

"ID, how old do you need to be to get a room? I'm over twenty one, I assure you, but it's nice for you to ask the question," I smile. That's why the Four Seasons are rated one of the best hotel chains in the world, customer service like that, you guys!

"No, miss."

"Oooh, miss." I smile again. My cheeky side is coming out.

"We cannot check you in without any identification." Bollocks. I turn to Faye and Rhonda. They are no longer at my side. Faye is asleep, curled up on the telephone booth chair and Rhonda is asleep on the couch by the glass table with the huge fuck off flower display.

"Just a minute," I say, as I stagger over. "Faye, Faye," I am shaking her now. "Have you got any ID?"

"No, no, I's don't want to, stop it," comes the response. I grab her handbag but there is only a lipstick and a tampon. I move to Rhonda and then realise she has no handbag. Did she even bring one out? That is something I am going to have to deal with later, not now. Now we need to get a room to sleep in, since there is a blizzard outside.

By this point, I have started to sober up a little. Fear can do that. Having looked outside and having no idea where we are staying, I realise that if we cannot get a room here, we won't get a room anywhere. Well, not one that's safe, anyway. We've all watched *Hostel* and there is no way I will be staying in a three star hotel in Eastern Europe.

I put on my best smile and saunter over to the reception desk. By now, another male has joined the desk.

"Well, it's like this, you see. I don't actually have any ID on me, but if you allow me to log onto my Facebook account, you can see that that's me and just print out my profile page, surely that will do as ID, won't it? A smile. We are getting somewhere.

"I'm afraid, miss, your profile picture on Facebook is not considered suitable ID. I cannot check you in without it."

Panic.

"But there is a blizzard out there, you cannot throw us out on the streets." My voice has gone up an octave.

"Miss, did you not think to make a reservation before you came over here?"

"Of course we did, I'm not stupid! I just can't remember where we are staying."

"Aah, how about I give you the names of some hotels in the area."

"You could read the entire lot and it would make no difference, I have no idea where we are staying."

"A key, miss, do you have the key?"

Brilliant! Of course, the key will have the hotel name on it, surely. I pull out a white plastic credit card type key. There is not even a smudge on it. Now I'm really starting to panic. Quick, think.

"But I'm a regular user of the Four Seasons, I should be on your mailing list," I manage to think up, praying that at some point in my life I have registered myself on the mailing list of the Four Seasons, despite the fact that I've never even stepped through the door of one before. But wait, surely Pete must have done so, what with all that time he spends registering to every fucking membership he can, in order to win some prize or nights stay, he must have registered us at some point?

He takes my details and taps the computer. "I'm sorry, miss, we have no record of you."

"But you can't send us out on the street, we will die." I make a fake weep rather dramatically. I'm moving into Oscar territory now.

"Perhaps there is someone we can telephone who might know," he politely asks, as he is now joined by another male behind the desk. I am starting to feel a bit outnumbered here. I look around. Faye lets out a belch. If I don't act quickly, we are going to be thrown out.

"Pete, I need to ring Pete, he can scan over my driving licence." I give the man our home number and the phone rings. It is on loud speaker. At first the answer machine kicks in. "Try again, please," I request.

At last, a rather groggy sounding Pete answers the phone.

"Hello, Mr Pete, my name is Arman and I am the reception manager at the Four Seasons in Prague. I have your wife with me, can I put her on?" Silence. It is obviously taking some time to digest.

"Pete, Peter, it's me. Jess."

"What? Who? Jess, is that you?"

"Of course it's me, how many Jesses do you know? I need you to scan over my driving licence."

"You need a what? Is this some kind of joke? It's like three thirty in the morning."

"Pete, I need you to focus, I need my driving licence."

Silence.

"Pete? Peter are you there?"

"Jess, what the fuck are you doing? Where are you?"

"I'm at the Four Seasons and I need you to scan over my driving licence."

"What the fuck are you doing at the Four Seasons?"

"It's a long story, can you fax over my driving licence please?"

I can hear the duvet being thrown bag and the sound of Pete's bones cracking. He's getting out of bed. Good, we are making progress. He's back on the line.

"Just tell me again why you need your driving licence?"

FFS!

"Oh, Peter, just send over my licence, will you? There is a blizzard, it's cold, I cannot check in, I have a purse full of cash and they won't let me give it to them."

Silence again. Arman takes the phone off me. I think he can see I am not helping the situation.

"Good morning, Mr Pete. Your wife has forgotten where she is staying and would like to stay here for the night, but in order to check her in we require some identification. I am afraid it is company policy."

Arman hands me the phone back and tells me he would like to speak to me.

"For fuck's sake, Jess, are you on your own?"

Here we go.

"No, Peter, I am with Faye and Rhonda. I am not stupid."

Silence.

"I think we will re-evaluate that later," says Pete. "Don't Faye and this Rhonda person know where you are staying?"

Tricky, I don't want to land Faye in the shit with Ian.

"Faye is, erm, sleeping right now."

"Well fucking wake her."

"I did."

"And?"

"And, well, she can't remember either."

"Fucking hell, Jess, what about this Rhonda?"

"Well, I'm not actually sure she is part of the group."

Silence – again. Arman is starting to look less hospitable.

"Look, we can stay up all night having this discussion if you like, Peter, or you can just fax over my licence and we can discuss the rest in the morning.

I can hear him moving, there is some loud banging going on. I hear the bleeping to the safe and some tapping.

"What's the email?"

"I'll put you back onto Arman."

I hand the phone over, pleased to end this conversation, for now anyway. Arman gives the email. "285.00 Euros," I hear Arman say. Bollocks. The phone is passed back to me. Shit.

"Pete, I told you, I don't know where we are staying, there is a blizzard outside and you cannot expect me check into a three star hotel." I am whimpering a little now.

"Jess, think where are you staying."

"I have no idea, Peter, just scan the bloody licence over."

"Put Arman back on."

Arman politely picks up the phone and nods, taps on his computer. By now, a few more staff have gathered into the reception area. The night cleaners are hovering just under Rhonda's feet. There is then a delay. Arman remains with the phone to his ear. Good old Pete, he must be digging out the licence and scanning it over. I will be tucked up in no time. Maybe even have a little night cap to celebrate.

"Ah, thank you and good night to you, sir." Arman puts the phone down.

"Has he sent it over?" I eagerly ask.

"No, miss, your husband has found details of where you are saying." He then says something in Czech to his colleague, who picks up the phone and I recognise something which sounds like taxi.

"Miss, we have arranged a taxi to take you back to your hotel."

Two minutes later, the taxi is here. I thank the team at the Four Seasons, shake my friends and drag them into the taxi. Within seconds, we are outside a hotel. I don't even have time to put on my seat belt. I recognise the exterior. Yes, this is it. A little disappointed, we enter the flat at the top of the hotel and try and sneak in as quietly as possible.

"Where the fuck have you been?" asks a very pissed off Leigh.

"The Four Seasons," is all I can manage. I stagger to our room and flop down on the bed.

When I eventually open my eyes, I am faced with two huge tits on the single bed opposite. Faye is massaging them, spraying some white stuff into a cup. "What the hell?" I ask, trying to focus.

"I forgot to bring my breast pump," replies Faye. She is still feeding her ten month old. "My tits are pounding." Poor Faye. She no longer looks quite as glam. Her hair is stuck up and her tits look red raw.

"Shall I get a hot towel?" I ask, being the only thing I can think might help right now. Either that or I offer to suck on them, but I fear the taste of breastmilk with this hangover might just make me vomit. She nods so I fetch a towel I've soaked under the hot water tap. The apartment is empty, the girls must have gone out. I look at the clock and see it's after one p.m. Oops, weren't we supposed to be all going out for lunch?

"How did we get home last night?" asks Faye.

"You don't remember the Four Seasons?"

"Four Seasons? What about the Four Seasons?"

As I explain the events of the previous evening, we both start giggling. Rhonda, where's Rhonda? I quickly scan the apartment bedrooms, in the last one I check there is a heap of duvet and tucked neatly under it is Rhonda, snoring her head off. Phew. She has also missed lunch. I later find out Rhonda joined us later, having flown out from Birmingham airport.

Since Faye is in so much discomfort, I decide we need to hit the streets to see if she can purchase a breast pump before she ends up with mastitis. I leave a note for Rhonda and we hit the streets. As we walk along, I decide I ought to check my phone. There are five missed calls from Pete and six text messages:-

"You back at the apartment?" 03.48

"Jess, you there?" 03.55

"FFS, Jess, answer your phone." 04.00

"I'm going to bed, just text me, will you?" 04.30

"Call me." 06.10

"Spoken to Leigh. Thanks for letting me know you are back safe."

Oh shit. There are two voicemail messages. I'm not sure I can handle listening to those right now. I send a quick text apologizing, saying my battery had died and I will call later. My hangover cannot cope with a grumpy, tired Pete right now.

Faye and I take to the streets of Prague in search of a breast pump. Not quite what I had in mind for our girlie weekend away, but needs must! We pass the lovely little boutique shops. I was about to suggest we go in a couple on our way to wherever it is we are heading, but Faye is grunting and oohing to a point where passersby are giving us a wide berth. Get the breast pump, find a nice looking bar so she can pump her tits somewhere, and then we can get back on track. The shops can wait for now.

Clearly, Eastern Europeans have no need for breast pumps. Two hours later, sore feet from them damn cobbled streets, which I initially found rustic and quaint, passing every shop, chemist, doctors surgery imaginable, no-one sells breast pumps. Now, for any budding entrepreneurs out there, there could be a real market for them, or you won't sell a single breast pad. After wandering aimlessly for what seemed like FOREVER, there is only one option left: the supermarket. How many times have you been abroad and thought to yourself, 'What a brilliant idea, a supermarket that sells everything.' Literally everything, you can buy a car, house, horse, child... surely in Eastern European supermarkets they must sell breast pumps? We go straight to the baby aisle. Suddenly, Faye has moved from oohh aaahhing to full blown labour. It sounds as if she is either having an orgasm or losing a limb. As we look down the baby aisle, I'm not really sure we are in the baby aisle, there is very little there. Baby shampoo, baby soap, one shelf of nappies and a few bibs. WTF? We must be down the wrong aisle. We are in Eastern Europe, after all, have I mentioned that? I head to the milk aisle, the only sensible aisle I can think of, but, surprisingly, there is just milk, whose milk I'm not sure, as there are quite a few random pictures of animals I never knew gave milk.

I ask the assistant. Of course, the language is a barrier so I have to use actions to get the message through. It's an interesting game of charades and, as you can probably imagine, it did not go well. Faye was making noises like a cow in labour whilst I was squeezing my tits. When I leaned in pretending to suck Faye's tits (like a baby, of course), that was a step too far. When those nice looking security guards arrived, I felt it was time to leave.

As we reach the cold cobbles of Prague, Faye says the paracetamol has kicked in. Being the strong hard Northern type she is, she insists we need to carry on with our day. It's well after three p.m. Prague time and by now my hangover is something slightly in the past. Now is a good time to call Pete. It rings but there is no answer. I try again and again but still no-one answers. For a split second I swap shoes: he's in Prague, I am at home with Davina, he called me in the middle of the night – no, stop it, I wouldn't have answered the phone at that ridiculous time in the morning. I leave a very humbling message.

"Hi, darling (I never call him darling), hope you guys are okay. Sorry we haven't spoken yet today, I miss you both, love you…"

I put the phone back in my bag, if anyone rings, even PPI, I am going to answer, I swear.

Chapter Eight
Prague Part Two

Since we've given up on the breast pump, we decide it's time to re-group. Faye texts Leigh to see where they are. "Wondered when you going to join us. We are in Trotters, over the bridge, first bar on your left." She sounds pissed off. Then again, it is three in the afternoon, after all, and we go home tomorrow. Faye and I agree not to mention just how shitfaced we got last night and to pretend we are totally up for tonight's outing. When we find the bar, all the girls are there, including Rhonda. Leigh insists we both have a shot, our punishment for turning up so late. The very thought makes me want to vomit but I cannot face getting into anyone else's bad books. As the Jagermeister is placed in front of me, I vomit a little in my mouth. Faye looks to the heavens and downs it in one. She turns a little green. I can't do it. I'm overthinking it. Leigh is glaring at me. It's as though this shot is a symbol of our friendship and if I don't drink it, it means I don't care. I try to imagine I am on *I'm a Celebrity Get Me Out of Here*, pretend there is £100,00 in it for me. I pick it up and down it. It burns down the back of my throat. I will it to stay down there, along with the other cocktails etc. I had last night. *Stop it. Don't think about it*, I say to myself. Food. I need food. Rhonda has ordered something, the others ate earlier. I check the menu, it's all pork and beef, neither of which I am particularly keen on. Why couldn't there be a chicken burger with big fat chips and onion rings, that would sort me out. I opt for the snitznel. The waiter asks if I want creamed cabbage with that. I vomit a little again in my mouth.

After I finish my unsatisfying lunch and three shots later, I start to feel a little human again, or maybe I'm just numb and unable to feel a thing. It's at this point I check my phone again. Bollocks. I have two missed calls from Pete. I excuse myself and step outside. I ring the home phone, knowing Pete is likely to answer since it's tea time and he will be getting Davina's tea ready.

"Hello."

"Hi, it's me."

There is a pause.

"Oh, hi," he replies.

"What you doing?" I ask, desperate to avoid talking about the early hours.

"Well, I'm making Davina's tea, putting her to bed, then probably off to bed myself since I got bugger all sleep last night."

Oh shit. Here we go.

"Well, I just wanted to, you know, check in and check you guys are okay and say, you know, thank you for helping last night."

"Helping? Jess, what kind of moron goes out without knowing where she is staying?"

Ouch, that hurts a little.

"Well I just assumed everyone else…"

"You just assumed everyone else knew. Yeah, well, that's great, except everyone else went back to the apartment except you and Faye."

"And Rhonda," I add, like it will make a difference.

"You know what Faye is like, I find it really concerning you could get yourself into that situation. I mean, you've got a child at home, for fuck's sake."

What's that got to do with it? She was still at home.

"I don't think it affected Davina, it's not like I'd have not got details of where I was staying if she was with me."

"What I mean, Jess, is you are supposed to be a responsible adult and after last night, well, what can I say?"

I am starting to feel a little pissed off. I am still on my mini break with the girls and he is starting to make me feel crap.

"Look, I made a mistake, it won't happen again. I'm sorry."

Silence again.

I feel the question burning inside me, I have to ask. "Was it because it was the Four Seasons? I know you've always wanted to stay there."

"No, Jess, it has nothing to do with which fucking hotel you picked, it has everything to do with your safety."

"Well, I'm safe," I reply.

"Great. See you tomorrow."

He hangs up. The bastard actually hangs up on me. *Well, fuck you.* I walk back into the bar and order eight more shots. He's not going to spoil my weekend away.

We all head back to the apartment in the hotel to get ready for our big night out. As I said earlier, Leigh has a nickname of Princess. I don't really feel I need to explain how she acquired this nickname, save that she has all the attributes of a demanding princess. Think The Little Princess, as in the cartoon character played by Jane Horrocks, combined with Veruca Salt, that's Leigh. She knows there is a theme but has no idea what it is. Whilst the others get ready, we stick her in the lounge alone to wait until we are ready to get her dressed. When we are all ready, we tell her to place on the blind fold and enter the lounge. She has to guess the theme. First, out come Faye and I in our matching Marie Antoinette costumes, supposedly the ugly sisters but actually rocking this look. The white stockings make my legs look amazing and who knew I suited a white curly wig.

Leigh stares. "You two look great," she forces herself to say. "Is it some kind of 17th Century theme?" I am impressed she got the right century.

"No," I tell her.

Faye calls out the next. Lou, dressed as a very beautiful Prince Charming, wearing a blue crushed velvet tunic with belt and royal red cape, steps into the room. Leigh looks puzzled, so I ask for the next. Out comes Bridget. She's wearing a 1950s style brown suit, holding a wand. It takes a second but then I realise, she's the fairy godfather. I laugh.

"Well done," I tell her.

Leigh is starting to look a bit pissed off. The variety of outfits is now blowing her mind. It's Rhonda's turn next, she's wearing a fabulous 1940s dress with deep red lips and heavy eye make-up. She looks awesome.

"Okay, so it's definitely a fashion era theme," says Leigh. She's perked up. I think she thinks she going to be wearing some kind 1920s flapper dress. There is giggling from the corridor, in come the three mice. All three are wearing the same sexy mini mouse costume. Each have a pair of fishnet holdups with red bows on the top, a red and white spotted skirt, black corset and a choker around their necks (that could come in handy later), a black painted nose and some black ears on a head band with a large red bow in the middle. They pretend to eat cheese. God, they are so annoying. I can tell Leigh is bored of looking at us all in our fabulous costumes, I have to say, we look like something that's come out the West End, from some kind of raunchy show – except Bridget, of course. Faye makes Leigh sit and tells her we need to do her make up first. She is kind and puts on the Touche Eclat and face powder, she gives her eyes a smoldering look, then proceeds to smudge in black across her cheeks – cinders, of course. Lou and Faye help Leigh into her costume, it's a rags gypsy style dress with criss cross bodice and raggy patches. It's just above the knee and Faye tightens the bodice so her tits look enormous. She still looks pretty, but I have a sneaking feeling she isn't going to be happy.

When we take her to the mirror, she stares at herself for a good couple of minutes, eyeing herself from side to side. "I'm Cinderella, aren't I?" she asks. We nod. Then come the tears. Cue mice. The three bumbling blondes fuss about Leigh. Faye and I exchange glances. Bridget couldn't give a toss, she's reading *Bolts and Nuts Magazine*. Lou is tidying up. The mice guide Leigh into their bedroom. Five minutes later, out comes a slightly more fresh face looking Leigh. Her hair is beautifully curled in ringlets, the smouldering look has been reduced to a more sparkly look and her bodice has been loosened to show off her breasts. It works. Now, I know some of you may wonder, why go to all this effort and not just buy the 'L' sign and stick some condoms on her head, but I like to pretend we think outside the box. The whole dressing up thing started on Lou's hen night, when we were all members of the YMCA. We had such a laugh, bursting into song at random times in the evening as though we had Tourette's. At any time, any one of us just needed to shout YMCA and we would have to re-group, sing and dance. It was fun, although you probably had to be there.

The three mice make us drink a shot of some odd looking vodka. Personally, I hate the stuff, but since I am probably old enough to be their mother, I down it. I swear I could breathe fire after that. Now that we are ready, it is time to hit the streets of Prague again. However, this time it's going to be a steadier night.

We are dropped off by the taxi driver on the main boulevard. It is filled with people. As we get out of the two taxis people are staring. A crowd is forming. People actually think we have come fresh from a show. Some guys come over and ask to have their picture with us. I pretend not to like this but, truth be told, I'm fucking loving it. A random stranger, who is easy on the eye, actually wants his picture with me. Even Bridget gets her fair share. Thirty minutes later, we are able to leave the spot from where we were dropped off. We head for the nearest bar. As we walk in, we get a few whistles and glares but, after that, no-one is particularly bothered. There are no tables to sit at so we all grab a bar stool and sit at the bar whilst we wait for our drinks. Now, if I was an artist, this would have made a great painting to hang over the toilet. You know how some people have dogs in clothing playing snooker? Well, eight women dressed up in burlesque style costumes, leaning over the bar, is quite a picture. There is no conversation between us. What do you say? The three mice are still giggling and the truth is, I actually just want to go to bed. It's not happening in here so I suggest we leave. I approach the barman, who I swear has been making fuck me eyes at me all night.

"So, where is the place to go?"

He looks shiftily around like he's telling me the code to the Crown Jewels.

"I get off in in about three hours, I'll be at '00'." He makes a symbol with his hands as the same time.

Sounds exciting, I think to myself. Not knowing quite what to make of this, I leave the bar with the rest of my comedy act. We walk around for a good ten minutes, looking from bar to bar to see if there is a vibe that will draw us in, and then I see it: '00'. The sign is above the door. There are men in suits outside looking quite official. I decide we should try anyway. At the point where I think a hand will be held up to stop us from going any further, I realise I am through the door. I look behind to see if anyone else has been let through and discover the whole group is in. Brilliant. I scour the surroundings. There is a DJ in the corner, next to a small dance floor, a bar that's lit up like Blackpool illuminations and several booths where you can only see the back of heads. As we walk forward, by chance a booth becomes available and we instantly stick our arses straight in it.

An attractive twenty-ish looking girl comes over to take our order. I'm starting to feel we are somewhere a little special here. How did we manage this? Is it because word got around they decided they needed to contain this weird looking group, or did the barman in the previous bar pull us some strings? As I am sat contemplating all of this, the music notches up a beat and the mice have hit the dance floor. Soon after Leigh follows, who drags Lou, who drags, Faye who drags me. All that is left in our booth is Bridget and Rhonda, but I'm not worried we will lose our seats. You've got to be brave to mess with the Fairy Godfather.

We are dancing. I am actually starting to really enjoy myself. Despite not knowing all the songs, there are a few I recognise. I am starting to relax and begin to let myself go. I begin to pull out my best moves, I am shimmying right down to the floor with my newly toned legs. I think of Pete as I am dancing, I realise he hasn't paid me a single compliment about my new physique. I realise I am quite hurt by this – this and his chastising. As I shimmy back up again, a short bearded guy, who looks about fifty, walks over to me.

"Lovin the costumes, honey, what you guys been in?"

He's American, I love Americans.

"It's just a hen night," I reply, shimmying down again.

"Y'all look amazing in those outfits."

"Thanks," I say as I shimmy back up again.

I turn and start dancing with Faye. I'm not sure what to make of this guy. After all, American's are such a mixed bag. I watch as the short bearded guy heads over to the bar and talks to another group of men. It's time for a drink. Faye and I head over to the booth. The rest remain. Rhonda and Bridget are sat in the booth and they seem to be getting on extremely well, perhaps a little too well, some might say. (Piercing appreciation must fall within the realms of lesbianism?).

I pour Faye and me the dregs of the bottle of prosecco. To be honest, I am not disappointed it's all gone; my mouth is starting to dry up. Faye asks what I want to drink. I really just want to say a Coke, full fat, but I know this won't go down well.

"Barcardi and coke," leaks from my lips.

Faye saunters off to the bar. She's there a while. I am feeling a little out of place sat with Bridget and Rhonda. They are making no effort to make me feel comfortable. In fact, the downright opposite, as Rhonda hoists her skirt up to show the dragon tattoo crawling down her thigh. Faye is taking an awful long time at the bar. Eventually she returns, without any drinks in her hands, but closely followed by three men and a bucket of champagne. The bearded American is with her. He smiles at me like we are old friends.

"Jess, Jess. Right, this is Tanner." She points to a tall handsome looking man. "This is Harrison." Another equally as good looking man, but a tad shorter. "And this is Bill. Guess what they do?"

"Astronauts?" I ask. It has to be something spectacular, although Bill looks a little to plump – maybe he's back from an expedition and going for it.

"Bloody Hollywood producers," she shouts, beaming from ear from ear like she has just caught herself a shark.

"Yeah, right, and I'm a dolphin trainer," I reply.

Tanner laughs.

"Seriously, Jess, just Google them." As I contemplate this, she shoves her phone under my nose: there is a picture of the three of them stood on the red carpet to the Premiere of *The Moon Has Fallen*. I read a bit of the blurb. Tanner and Harrison are the producers, Bill is the director. I scroll down a little further and read "TH Wright Productions have hit Hollywood by storm. With more than ten box office hits and a turnover of over twenty five million dollars last year..." I read no more. Enough is said.

"Hi," I say, standing up to properly introduce myself, forgetting I am in costume. I shake hands with Tanner and Harrison, Bill gives me a kiss on the cheek.

Tanner leans in. "I love your costume. Faye says you are on a hen weekend."

"Yes, obviously I don't normally dress like this."

"Of course not," he smiles, "You could hardly come out in your wetsuit."

I look at him questioningly.

"I assume you wear a wetsuit when working with the dolphins?" He smiles, I smile. "So, what do you do, when not training dolphins?"

"Well, obviously that keeps me very busy. Flipper is very demanding. But other than that, I am a full time mother and wife," I say, lowering my voice slightly on the wife part. "I used to be the head of marketing for a chocolate factory, but I had to travel a lot and when Davina was born, it just wasn't workable." Tanner nods understandingly. "You know, I always wanted to work in television, films particularly. I wanted to be a make-up artist, I even went to beauty college, just never got my big break."

"Well, you know the right people now, don't you?" He smiles. He's got lovely teeth and lovely eyes and his voice, it's so, so American and sexy.

"So, what are you doing in Prague?" I ask.

"We are filming, we have been here for two weeks now, we are just finishing off this week and then we head back to L.A."

Wow. That just sounds so, L.A., I love it.

"Ooh, what are you filming, who's in it?"

"Well, I can't give specifics, but certainly someone you will have heard of."

This is so exciting, just the thought that he has been sat next to, probably had coffee with, an A lister Hollywood superstar is the most amazing thing I can imagine. He pours me some more champagne. It tastes great, everything is great. When Leigh, Lou and the three mice appear, I become slightly irritated. I don't want to share. Thankfully Tanner doesn't even look at them, his eyes are on me. Faye and Harrison are in deep conversation and Bill has started chatting to some girl at the bar, having gone to get more champagne. "Come on, ladies, it's time to move on," says Leigh. *Like fuck it is.* I'm not going anywhere.

"Oh, er, Bill has just gone to get us another drink, why don't we catch you up?" I glance at Faye for some backup.

"Yeah, we'll catch you up." Faye turns and carries on her conversation with Harrison.

"Well, we don't know where we are going to go yet."

"Yep, that's fine," I respond, not listening to a word she is saying. Tanner is telling me about their last movie, filmed in Antarctica.

"I said, we don't know where we are going yet," says a rather pissed off Leigh.

"Well, just text us and we will find it."

"Fine, come on, girls," says Leigh to the rest. Bridget and Rhonda make no attempt to move. Leigh snatches her jacket, the mice don't have one, and storms out of the bar.

Lou is looking a little weary and I feel bad for her but sod that, back to Tanner.

As the night whizzes by, I realise I've been talking to Tanner for a good two hours. We know everything about each other. He has a wife and they have a daughter who is eighteen months. They, of course, have a full time nanny. His wife is an actress but struggling to get a lead role, which is causing some friction in their marriage. I tell Tanner how lost I feel at present, not knowing which direction to turn. I need something, but aren't sure what it is, and Pete just doesn't seem to understand me anymore. Tanner sympathises. He understands. It's like he knows me, and did I mention he has lovely eyes? Faye and Harrison are on the dance floor, having a smooch. Bill is snogging some girl at the bar. I can see his tongue swarming around the poor girl's mouth. Further along in the booth, Bridget and Rhonda are kissing. I nudge Tanner and we giggle. Bridget spots me laughing; she and Rhonda make a quick exit. It's just Tanner and me in the booth now. Suddenly, my heart starts pounding. He places his hand on my knee and I feel a fire beginning to rise in my stomach. Tanner removes some of the synthetic hair from your mouth.

"Can I see your real hair?"

Shit. God knows what it looks like.

"I'll be back in a sec."

I head to the toilet and take off my wig. My hair is flat to my head, but after a quick blow under the hand dryer, it gets a bit of life back in it. It's not great, but it's not too bad either. As I check myself in the mirror and reapply my lipstick, Pete creeps into my head. He was so moody earlier, I'm not doing anything wrong, just chatting. I need some fun right now. I decide to put Pete to the back of my mind.

As I walk out of the bathroom, Tanner takes a double take. I check behind me to see if he is looking at someone else but then I realise, he's looking at me. As I walk back to the booth, he gently pulls my arm towards him.

"God, you are beautiful," he says. He leans in and kisses me on the lips. I don't respond. He pulls back and looks directly into my face, seeking approval to carry on. I part my lips and he gives me the most sexiest, lip curling, nail biting kiss. He kisses me – a proper movie style kiss. I have a serious wide on right now. Harrison and Faye re-join us to have a drink. They are holding hands. Uh-oh. Well at least we are partners in crime.

"Harrison and I are going to take a walk," says Faye.

I decide it's time for a meeting in the toilets. As I enter, Faye lets out a little scream.

"Oh my God, Jess, how sexy are they? I'm going back to his hotel…"

"Faye," I say, becoming concerned that this is going a little too far, "are you going to shag him?"

"I don't know yet."

"But what about Ian and the kids?" Faye looks at me disapprovingly.

"You know Ian had an affair three years ago. Call it payback. Anyway, I honestly think if he knew he was a Hollywood producer he would approve."

I nod, this makes complete sense. It's like the promise Pete and I made years ago. I promised Pete that if Demi Moore ever threw herself at him he had my permission to shag her, just like I had his permission to shag Patrick Dempsey, should he ever try it on. In fact, I should ask if he knows Patrick.

"Look, just take care, okay? Text me where you are staying, we need to get our story straight before Leigh puts two and two and makes six."

Faye and Harrison leave the bar; she promises to text as soon as she gets to his hotel. We agree to meet up later, to arrive back at the apartment together having been to an all night club.

It's just Tanner and me. We decide to go for a walk around Prague. It's snowing a little outside. Right now, with Tanner, I feel whole again. We are surrounded by beautiful buildings and architecture lit up; it looks like a fairy tale. We are holding hands and I don't have a care in the world right now. As we wander down the cobbled streets together, Tanner stops and kisses me again, the same passionate Hollywood type kiss. My knees are knocking, a shiver is running up and down my spine. God, I think I am in love.

"Jess, will you come back to my room?" he asks when our mouths finally untwine. I can't speak, I can't think, which is a good thing right now. I nod. We walk a little further together until we get to the, wait for it, Four Seasons. Bollocks. Not here again.

"Erm, do you have your key?" I ask.

"Of course I do," says Tanner, pulling out the plastic key card from his pocket, looking at me quizzically. Phew, at least I won't need to go anywhere near reception. Luckily, it's just off to the left from the lobby. As I walk into The Four Seasons, Tanner firmly has my arm. He leads me straight in and straight over to reception. "Can you send up some champagne and do you want something to eat, Jess?" he asks.

The receptionist looks up, "Ah, Mrs Jess, good to see you again."

Fuck. It's Arman again from last night.

"I trust you arrived back to your hotel safely this morning?" I nod. Tanner is looking at me.

"Mr Pete did ring us about an hour or so after you left to check you had gone. He said he had been trying to call you."

"It's a long story," I tell Tanner.

"Sorry, sir, champagne, you say, and Mrs Jess, would you like something to eat in the room?" I swear he said room with a judgemental tone.

"No I'm fine," I say. *Get me out of here.*

Tanner leads me to the lift. "What was all that about?" he asks, slightly accusatory.

As we enter the lift, I explain about last night. He doesn't look entirely convinced, he probably thinks I was here with another man. Shit, my dreamy, Hollywood romance is evaporating, real life is re-emerging and I don't like it. Tanner seems a little more distant. As we enter his suite, there is a sudden awkwardness between us. I sit out the couch in one of the sitting rooms, I can just make out the bedroom, which has a massive fuck off bed. Tanner sits next to me. He leans straight in to kiss me but this time the kiss is different, it is not as passionate, it's a little more forceful and not in a good way. I pull back. The doorbell rings. Saved by the bell. Tanner gets up and collects the champagne bucket from the bellboy, giving him a massive twenty dollar tip. The Americans are so generous. He comes back over to the settee and pours us both a glass of champagne. My mouth has gone dry again. That fuzzy feeling I had before is now turning into a headache. We both sit there in silence. The mood has gone. We have nothing to talk about. The silence is unbearable.

"Look," I say, placing my barely touched champagne glass on the coffee table. "Tonight has been great, I mean, really special, but it's just, you know…"

"I know, the fire has gone."

Steady on there, I think to myself, *I'm still hot, right?* Tanner's phone pings. It's a message from Mrs Tanner with a picture of their daughter. We exchange looks; he suddenly feels really uncomfortable, I can tell.

"Shall we just call it a night?" I ask. There is disappointment in my tone.

"It's up to you, unless we just have a shag and then call it a night?" he asks. I begin to wonder if this was all an act.

"I think perhaps not," I reply.

"Shall I ask reception to call you a cab?"

"No, it's okay, the hotel is literally just around the corner."

"I'll walk you round," he says. I'm surprised he's offered – perhaps it wasn't just about a shag after all. "You can't walk alone, it's not safe." Bless him. Such a good guy, Pete would like him – although it's probably best not to tell him the hot American millionaire producer walked me back to my own hotel after we had been in his suite.

As I walk down the lobby, I stick my head around the corner into reception to see if Arman is there – it's important he sees me leave. He's not there. *Shit.*

"Tell Arman Jess says bye."

Some snotty looking woman just nods back at me. I'm not too worried, it is highly unlikely I will be staying in the Four Seasons in the near future.

As I get to my hotel, Tanner takes hold of my hand. "I've had one of the best nights, Jess," he says. "Perhaps things worked out for the best after all. Good luck with everything." He leans in and gives me a gentle kiss on the lips. I can't speak. I don't want him to go. I feel like I need him again. I can feel tears in my eyes welling. "Goodnight, Jess."

He walks away, leaving me stood in the lobby. God, why does it hurt to see him walk away, I barely know him? What was it that I wanted, needed, what was he offering that made me feel so wanted? I don't know. I just know that I don't feel special anymore, far from it. As I walk towards the lift in reception, it suddenly dawns on me that I need to wait for Faye or else she will be busted with Leigh. It's 01.30 in the morning. I text her. No reply. There is an old message saying, "OMG, back at the Four

Seasons, suite this time, more accommodating than the telephone booth! Don't be good ;-) xx." I go and sit in the bar; there is no-one there, it's all closed up. I grab myself a chair and sob. I am not really sure why I am sobbing but I feel empty. Without realising, I drop off to sleep.

I wake up to someone shaking me. "Jess, Jess, wake up."

Fuck, my neck hurts, my back hurts. I'm curled up in a ball in the seat. Faye is stood in front of me, disheveled looking, with mascara down her cheeks. It takes me a minute to focus. I check my watch; it's 05.45.

"You okay?' I ask.

"Yeah, I'll tell you later, let's get back to the apartment, we've been to a club, right?"

"Right," I say.

As we get to the apartment, we open the door as quietly as we can and tiptoe into the bedroom. No-one is up, thank fuck. I climb into bed and fall into a deep sleep. I have the strangest dreams: one about bats flying at my face, wanting to suck on my cheeks, the other about a Golden Hair mermaid who gives birth to Pete, I'm watching the birth, Pete sees me and tells me I disgust him. WTF?

Faye and I are woken to a banging on our door. It's Lou.

"Guys, you need to get up, the taxi will be here in ten minutes to take us to the airport."

Shit. We both leap out of bed and scurry about, shoving everything into our bags. When we get to reception, everyone is looking a little jaded. Leigh, who clearly has the huff, tells us about this fantastic club they all went to where she was made to go on the stage and did some of her dance moves. I try to look impressed. Faye's expression is difficult to see, her dark sunglasses hiding most of her face.

Faye and I don't get chance to discuss the night before but a few days later, after we get home, we meet for a coffee. I tell Faye all about my whirlwind romance with Tanner. She gives me a blow by blow account of all the filthy sex she had with Harrison. Apparently he could go for hours, but turns out he wasn't that nice afterwards. Asked her to leave. He doesn't like to sleep with women, apparently. Faye holds no guilt. Ian put her through hell a few years ago. She says she feels vindicated and can now move forward. Whatever floats your boat, I guess. I would never judge, and she knows that.

Chapter Nine
Davina's Birthday

It's a Friday night. Pete isn't talking to me. When he walked down the driveway this evening with his new blonde streaks in his hair, I couldn't help but laugh. When I broke into a chorus of, "Flash, aha, Master of the Universe," he really didn't see the funny side.

"Fuck off," he said as he walked past, confirming he didn't appreciate my comedy mantra.

Davina is sat on Pete's lap, watching 'Grandpa in My Pocket'. Growing up in the 80s, if anyone asked you if you wanted to see a rocket in their pocket, you knew to run and scream! I'm tucking into my first glass of Pinot Grigio, okay, so maybe third, but who's counting? I'm flicking through Facebook and go to the 'My Memories' page. Ha, cute, Davina wearing her snow suit in June, aged four (the late snow shower – gotta love this country). The one of my veggie plot. Looks bloody brilliant, if I do say so myself. Mr Bloom would be proud. I blush at the thought! The next is Davina at Macy's Adventure Playground, 5th Birthday party – *aah, crikey, that must have been around a year ago? Fuck!* As if they know my thoughts, Pete and Davina look at me. I gently ease myself out of the lounge to go and check the diary in the kitchen. I am fairly certain her birthday is the 4th of

June, but best to check to be doubly sure. I check the calendar and there, in brightly coloured pen, is a big 'D bitherday' – expertly written by Davina. I start counting back. Erm, just two weeks, fuckety fuck. *How could I have let this happen? What kind of parent am I?* Okay, no time for self-judgment. I need a plan and I need it fast. Googling is always the best way to start, so I google 'six year old birthday party ideas'. Build a Bear pops up – brilliant. That'll do, who doesn't like to stuff some fluff in a hole? I check out our local Build a Bear, they have an online booking facility – genius. The next available slot is 12th August – fuckety fuck with a big fuck. Now, this is the part where I look at something like Netmum but, I'm sorry, the women who are posting on this site have clearly read every parenting book on the shelf. Their precious child's birthday was planned and booked the very next day after their last birthday. If only there was a site for 'Crap, I forgot it's my daughter's birthday in two weeks.' I did actually try to google that but all I got back was 'Is it normal?' and 'Is adoption the kindest thing?' Ideas, I need ideas. As a six year old, what would I have liked? A Cabbage Patch Kid and Ken to go with my Peaches in Cream Barbie, and I mean a proper Ken, not a cheap replica that looks like the twin of Ken who clearly didn't get enough of the placenta. I start thinking and the only thing I can think of is my rabbit (no, not that kind!), Bugsy Rabbit, my teddy. He was great. I remember spending my entire savings on him in Ibiza when I was six. I paid in potatoes; aahh, happy days. But I digress: rabbit, how can that help? I haven't the time to come up with some rabbit theme. Hang on, rabbit, time... bloody genius – Alice, oh, thank you, Alice, and your crazy Wonderland. Mad Hatter's Tea Party it has to be. I can pull this off in two weeks. I so can, look at Pete's 40th, that was a huge success.

I wander back into the lounge and remind Davina she needs to let me know how many she wants to come to her party.

"What party?" she asks. Doh!

"Your sixth birthday party," I remind her.

"Oh, I thought you'd forgotten."

I laugh, it sounds a bit evil. Pete and Davina stare at me.

"You know, for your Mad Hatter's Tea Party."

"I didn't ask for a Mad Hatter's Tea Party," is her response.

"Surprise."

Again with the stares.

"Daddy said we would go swimming and to Maccie D's."

Bollocks – so much easier.

"Ah, well, Daddy knew the plan."

"Really?"

Bless her response, staring now at her daddy, her doting father who would never lie. I'm glaring now, the kind of glare only woman can do.

"Er, yes, pumpkin," he says, glaring back but not as scary. "Mummy has had it all planned for weeks, she's even going to make a cake." Bastard! Pete knows my culinary skills are not advanced in the 'anything you need to add baking powder to' department.

"Thank you, Daddy," says Davina as she hugs Pete. *Excuse me, but wasn't this my idea?*

Davina is in bed. Pete comes down the stairs, having read the bed time story. My tongue is hovering around the neck of the bottle of Pinot Grigio. He wasn't supposed to see that.

"So, what's the plan, Lewis?"

Clever cock.

"Well, I'm thinking those great guys at 'Just Pop it Up' can set us up again."

"Jess, I've seen the credit card bill, it's a 6th birthday party, not a fucking wedding."

Okay, I was just thinking on my feet, I tell myself.

"Well, I thought we could put a tent of some kind in the garden and set a massive table. We can use the two wallpapering tables we've acquired." (One from his parents and the other I bought when I decided I was becoming an interior designer).

"And what if it rains?"

Awkward bastard.

"Well, we will just set it up in the garage."

"What's wrong with the house?"

Er, hello, just because I haven't bought any more cushions or floaty candles recently doesn't mean I mean don't actually give a shit.

"The dining room table isn't big enough." It's the best excuse I can come up with right now but it seems to be working as Pete is thinking.

"Well, I did see on Groupon a cheap pop up marquee for one hundred quid so I could get that." Brilliant.

"Don't worry, I'll sort the rest."

"Jess, I don't want you spending a fortune on this, just because you forgot."

I forgot – excuse me, I thought she had two parents? I'm at a crossroads here, do I get arsey and remind him she has two parents, or do I just get more Pinot Grigio, bearing in mind we fell out last night because we had run out of toilet paper? I decide, being the better person, that I will let this one pass.

"You get the tent, I'll get some blow up flamingos and a tea service." I smile and head to the kitchen for the Pinot.

Wow! I mean, *wow*. Just Google 'Mad Hatter's Tea Party' and see what it comes up with. That Lewis person sure knew what the future held. 'Eat me' and 'Drink me' labels are a massive hit on a bit of card. I thought they were only popular on a certain street in Amsterdam. As for the choice of blow up flamingos, well, who bloody knew? Since I am lacking in the time department (ironic, isn't it?), I order just about as much as I can. Amazon Prime is a wonderful thing. Everything will be arriving tomorrow. Now for the dinner service. Now that's a bit different. There is no such thing as a cheap dinner service. *Think, Jess. Think.* And then it occurs to me, I remember all those charity shops on the high street in Pocklington. The ones that, in addition to half completed tapestry, sell candles in tea cups. Perfect, the kids can drink blackcurrant juice out of china tea cups. You see, I'm not so bad at this parenting malarkey after all.

It's the day before the party. Pete has taken the day off and is putting up the cheap tent from Groupon. Luckily, there is glass between us so I can't hear his profanities. I am melting out the rest of the wax from the eighteen tea cups I bought. The shop assistant looked really pleased when I asked for all eighteen. I think she thought they'd created something ingenious, maybe modern day, candles in china. The truth is, the only reason anyone younger than fifty has china is because their mother-in-law bought it for them as a wedding present, or they are one of these vintage types who wears 1950s dresses and red lipstick and has Cath Kidston everywhere.

I can't complain. I was rather pleased with my purchases. All eighteen tea cups came with matching side plates. It was a bit of a mish mash but it just so worked. I was particularly pleased with the two cake stands I got from John Lewis. (They didn't have any in Pocklington's Oxfam or Help the Aged.) Everything was in order for the perfect Mad Hatter's Tea Party. Pete could blow up the flamingos in the morning and the crocket set would go out on the lawn. So that left the next biggest challenge, the cake. For the past couple of years I'd bought her birthday cake from Waitrose. She'd started to cotton on to the caterpillar from Tesco, so I had to up my game. Last year she had a jewel encrusted handbag. It was a sheer work of art and only cost £65.00. But, thanks to Pete, this year there would be no handbag or caterpillar:

it was going to be a Jess Special. For some reason, I chose not to look at a single cook book first. I decided I would just buy pretty much the contents of the baking aisle in Tesco and work back from there. Luckily, I had been bought a few cook books, subtle hints from my mother-in-law. I had Nigella, Gary, Gordon... I even had the Betty's Tea Shop cookbook. Everything was there, I just needed to measure out and bake and that's just what I did. I measured out, I poured in a bowl, I spread in a cake tin and placed in the oven. It smelt okay. This is easy. *Thanks, Nigella.* However, when I got it out it looked like a memory foam mattress. *What went wrong?* I checked the ingredients list: they must have missed something off. Baking powder? But I put that in. I pick up the baking powder tub, but realise it's actually bicarbonate of soda – why do they both look the same? Who does that? (For the record, I actually had to do this for research and a memory foam mattress is a good description, in my humble opinion). My cake needed depth and depth is what it would get. I decided to ignore Nigella and go it alone. What could add depth? I knew, marshmallows. I layered marshmallows on top of the inch thin cake. Problem was it looked like a memory foam mattress with too many scatter cushions. Chocolate. Saves every situation. I delicately melted some chocolate and poured it over the marshmallows. Brilliant, it covered the lot. Was it appetising? That wasn't the brief. The brief was a cake for Davina's birthday! It certainly fit the Mad Hatter's Tea Party theme.

After taking a step back, I realised it was quirky, a bit maddish, after all. There is only so much you can do. This is where Mr Kipling and his Fondant Fancies come in a treat. I built a table and chairs. By the time I finished, it looked like a small fort. I was running out of time. I improvised on the characters with Betty Crockett icing and stuck it in the fridge.

The next day, considering it was Davina's birthday, we barely spent any time with her. Pete was blowing up flamingos and I was laying the table. When she asked if she could help, she almost got her head bitten off. It's at this point I began to wonder who this party is actually for. Suddenly, the way the napkins are creased and how the deck of cards float from the ceiling actually really matters. It's like I'm actually good at this. The set-up, the food, the party, every parent wants to outdo the next. You lose what it's all about and suddenly this party represents how good a parent I am. As I complete the finishing touches, I stand back in awe. *Wow.* Alice would be very fucking proud. She'd eat whatever cake I brought her in this venue.

The sad thing about a children's party is the fact you have to then bring the children in. Within seconds, it's carnage. Cheesy balls are being fired like canons and there is blackcurrant juice split already over my Cath Kidston table cloth. One of the brats claims to have chipped a tooth on the bone china tea cups. I stand back. *Can this really be happening?* All this hard work (well, two weeks) has resulted in this. Before I lose it completely, I look at Davina: there she is, smiling from ear to ear, at the top of the table. I feel so proud when she calls out her first 'Off with his head.' I actually shed a tear. As one of the blown up flamingos farts its way past my head, having had the air let out, I realise this is what it's all about. As I smile to myself, Pete comes out the kitchen with something like a swamp in his hands. Oh, it's the cake. I've always wondered, what time at a children's party is it appropriate to open the prosecco? It is, after all, a party, and what's a party without bubbles? I think I have earned them. After Davina screamed at the sight of her cake, all that effort forced upon me, Pete produces a magical My Little Pony Cake (freshly baked by Waitrose). Why would he do that? It was a set-up, he's clearly still bitter about the Flash Gordon comment and probably still not forgiven me for Prague, but using our daughter as a pawn in the 'Punish Jess' saga is not okay.

As the parents arrive to collect their munchkins, I'm bouncing about the garden on a space hopper. What Pete fails to realise is that, five months ago, I wouldn't have been able to bounce anywhere other than on the spot, but since I've been pumping, the new muscles I have grown in my legs allow me to do this. After all the kids and parents have left, with their slice of My Pony and a party bag that knocks the socks off any other party bag – there are bunny ears, doily notepads, Haribo sweets, pack of cards, chocolate flamingos and an edible china tea cup – I decide to get into a blazing row with Pete.

"Thanks, thanks for sharing your purchase with me. I looked a complete tit producing my cake, why would you do that?"

"First off, the tit looking you did all by yourself. Bouncing about on a space hopper screaming 'I'm late, I'm late,' puts you into the tit category all on your own."

Nasty. I'm a little taken aback by this. This is clearly more than the Flash Gordon comment, something is brewing. *I've done something, think, what can it be?* Nothing. Of course, having now drunk a bottle of prosecco, I am not going to allow this crazy talk simply pass by. "I don't know what the fuck is going on with you."

"Sshh, Davina will hear you."

Bam. In the face. I try to lower my voice and start at the beginning again just to get the effect. "I don't know what the fuck is going on with you: first the hair, then the judging, you know what you married, you know what you got yourself into when you got with me." This isn't going the way I planned. "I am who I am, don't judge me." I shut my mouth. That was crap. Where was the venom in that? He looks at me and this is what really hurts, the look of disapproval. That hurts. My Pete never disapproved. Although he perhaps wasn't always the one joining me on the stage with the live band, rocking and rolling, he was always at the front clapping along. I can't contain it. The tears start bubbling out and, suddenly, I am a blubbering mess. Davina runs out from the lounge.

"Mummy, Mummy, what the matter?"

"Ask your daddy."

Cruel, bringing her into it, but I wasn't the one who produced a My Little Pony cake. I decide to take myself to bed. That will show him, he will be really worried that he's hurt me beyond repair.

When I wake up the next morning, he's already up. He's in the kitchen making breakfast for Davina, who isn't awake yet. What time did she go to bed last night? He saunters over, he's happy, he kisses me on the side of the cheek – I wasn't expecting that. He's playing mind games. This could be DefCon four.

"How you feeling?" he pipes up.

Erm, wasn't expecting this.

"I feel great," is all I can manage. I am confused. Wasn't the argument supposed to continue this morning? Wasn't he supposed to be worried he had upset me? I am not sure what this means. Since it's caught me by surprise, I simply pour myself a coffee and go up to see my daughter. I need a cuddle and some girlie time.

Chapter Ten
Agony Auntie Janet

As I pull into the car park at Junction 42 Shopping Centre, I'm not quite sure what to expect. I am meeting Auntie Janet today for a cuppa and a shop, but she knows me well and the fact I've not managed to disguise the bags under my eyes means something is going on. She might not be in tune with the kids, but she knows when there is trouble afoot.

I walk into the café. She's already sat there, writing a list. Auntie Janet likes to write lists. She has a list for everything, not just food shopping. She will have a list of everything she needs to achieve that day – put on slow cooker, get petrol, paint nails, etc. etc. As I enter the café, she looks up like she knew I was there before I knew I was there, if you follow. As we make eye contact, she instructs me to sit. Do not pass the coffee counter, do not look at the cakes, just sit. I do as instructed. I do not have the energy or willpower to challenge Auntie Janet today. As I sit in front of her, I feel my shoulders sag and for some reason I start to cry. Auntie Janet doesn't say a word. She gets up and walks over to the counter. "Americano, strong, black, and a large piece of that Devil's Chocolate Cake." Good old Auntie Janet. She always knows how to cheer me up.

Five minutes later she comes back with the coffee and the chocolate cake. The coffee is placed under my nose and she starts tucking into the cake. *WTF*. I start to stand to try and find some milk but I am instructed to sit down. Again, I don't have the strength to challenge her. A sob blurts out.

"I know what is wrong, Jessica Veronica (bloody grandmother!) Raynard."

Oh, so we are full naming, are we? I didn't come here for this.

"You are drinking too much."

I am immediately defensive – that's what alcoholics do, right?

"I'm not upset because I am drinking too much."

"Listen, you are drinking too much and it's affecting your marriage."

"That has nothing to do with it," I argue, perhaps a little too defensively.

"Yes it does, you are off and away on your girlie nights and weekends and parties and you aren't paying enough attention to your marriage."

Bloody hell, did Pete speak to her first?

"I'm paying plenty of attention," I find myself defending. "I'm the perfect housewife: I cook, clean, iron, look after Davina, Pete is not missing out at all. He's the one off on his work's dos and 'corporate' entertaining evenings."

"There is more to it than that, Jessica, and you know it."

I look back, pretending to be puzzled. The truth is I am puzzled, I don't know when or why it's going wrong, but it is.

"How's your sex life?"

I nearly spit out my vile cup of tar. 'WTF' is written all over my face.

"When did you last have sex?"

I look around. I swear she upped a notch when she said the word 'sex'.

"I don't think…"

"Oh, don't give me that shit, Jessica, and don't look at me like that either. Just because I don't lord it about now doesn't mean I didn't have a past. Before Colin died, we were at it like rabbits."

Fucking hell, I wasn't prepared for this.

"Answer the question, when did you last have sex?"

I start thinking. It's taking a while. I recently watched Magic Mike and was definitely up for it, it must have been around then… no, I remember now, we fell out because Pete said there was no valid storyline, it was just an excuse to show off their muscles. The fact I've been thinking about this hasn't gone unnoticed. "Too long. If you need to think about it and pull those faces, it's clearly been too long."

"Auntie Janet, I really don't feel comfortable discussing this sort of thing with you."

"Oh grow up," she retorts. "If you can go parading around in fancy dress looking like a hooker, wearing no more than a tarts knickers, you can talk to me about this. Now, listen, a good marriage is built on good foundations, in those foundations are the obvious building blocks: honesty, monogamy, the ability to communicate and regular sex. Men need it, Jessica, and they need it often, otherwise they will go and get it elsewhere."

Fucking hell! Where has this come from?

"Look, we do have sex, just not as often. It's not the sex, or lack of sex, that's the issue in our relationship, it's just, it's just..." I feel the tears welling up again.

Auntie Janet leans in and grabs my hand. Her voice is a tad softer. "All I'm saying, Jessica, is you need to spice things up a bit more. If he's happy in the bedroom, you will find you are happier in general. Men's moods are controlled by their cocks. I've said it before and I will say it again."

Fucking hell, I cringe to myself!

"It's a sad truth," she says, looking at my clearly pained stricken face. "Look, it's not just intercourse, a blow job has almost the same satisfaction. So long as you can suck it like you are sucking a golf ball through a hose pipe, he will be happy." I literally spit out my drink. The couple sat at the table next to us leave, they don't even finish their coffees or walnut cake. "Spice it up, Jessica, get some lingerie, buy some accessories..."

"Accessories, what kind of accessories?"

"You know, the vibrating type."

Holy cow, could this get any worse? Auntie Janet suggesting I buy a dildo – what next, a swingers group vacation...

"And you need to get away."

Did she hear me?

"Away?" I ask.

"Yes, away, just the two of you, I'll have Davina, you two need to spend some time together."

When I leave the café an hour or so later, it's all booked. Pete and I are getting the 8.30 a.m. train to London a week on Saturday. We are staying at the Holiday Inn and have managed to get a late sitting at a very well-known restaurant called The Vine. Once Auntie Janet raised the topic of a night away, I decided I wasn't so embarrassed to discuss our sex life after all. I've promised her I will hit Victoria's Secret in Meadowhall and get onto www.sluttywife.com when I get home.

Chapter Eleven
London, baby

I wake up early. I'm excited, so is Pete. We managed to get through the whole of last night without a single cross word. Both of us are looking forward to this weekend. Pete is particularly excited about the number of unlabeled boxes that have arrived this week. I packed my bag last night and bolted it shut. There are more locks on that holdall than a high security prison door. Even for me, the thought of having a cock ring, vibrator, nipple teaser and cock rub tub fall out of my luggage for all to see is too much to bear.

"Jesus, Jess, what you got in here?" Pete asks with a sly smirk. "I've locked my bag up and forgot to put in my aftershave."

"Put it in here," I suggest, offering my smaller tapestry bag with my cosmetics in.

The taxi arrives promptly and, before we know it, we are both sat on the train in First Class heading south. When the drinks trolley comes around, I resist the offer of a glass of fizz, not because it's only 9.15 in the morning but because I don't want anything to spoil this weekend. We both work out a plan of where we want to go. Pete loves museums and historical buildings. I don't, but it's about compromise – wasn't that one of the building blocks Auntie Janet mentioned? I agree to just the one museum, the Natural History Museum. At least I can replay Night at the Museum. Pete agrees that after lunch we can head to Oxford Street for a bit of light shopping and, if there is time, a quick visit to Harrods. One thing we did not need to agree on is our agreement to having a bottle of fizz in the Orient Hotel bar. This used to be a tradition each Christmas pre-Davina. We would get the train down for a day's Christmas shopping then have a bottle of fizz in the Orient whilst sussing out who was an escort and which one we would choose for a threesome. (Of course, we never did anything like that, but the thought was a turn on.)

When we disembark the train, Pete takes the bags and leads us out of the station. He passes the entrance to the tube, which takes me by surprise. He knows how much I hate the tube, the thought of being underground, packed in like sardines in a tin is scary stuff for me, but Pete has normally insisted, since travelling by any other means is simply a waste of time and money. However, today, he is leading us straight to the taxi rank. This pleases me. As I take a seat in the cab, I lean over and kiss him on the cheek. "Thank you," I say. Pete squeezes my leg and puts my hand in his. This is going to be a great weekend. *Thank you, Auntie Janet*, I say to myself.

After we've dumped our bags at the hotel, having told the concierge not to open my bag whatever happens, although having to backtrack slightly when he seemed to get a bit scared there might be an explosive in there, I whisper there is a birthday present for Pete and I don't want him to see it. The concierge, still looking a little concerned, agrees to ensure no-one tries to open it. We then hit the street. The Natural History Museum isn't far from the hotel and a walk on such a lovely day through the streets of London will be great, making me feel like I'm one of the locals.

Two hours later we emerge from the museum. Pete is carrying a plastic museum bag which contains a puppet T-Rex and a t-shirt bearing said same T-Rex for Davina. That's that box ticked, the rest of the shopping is mine. Pete is still buzzing from the amount of history he has absorbed in the last two hours. "You know what, Jess, if I could re-train I'd be an archaeologist. How cool would it be to dig up relics of the past?" The only thing I can think would be cool about that is wearing the khaki pants and hat and being in a hot climate, but I go along with him, not wanting to dampen his spirit.

Lunch; we need to eat. Suddenly I am famished. I could eat a horse right now and am definitely feeling in the mood for a little tipple; after all, it is 11.45 a.m. Pete tells me about a great bistro café he has read about called Portello. It's in the Notting Hill area. Perfect. Let's do it. He flags down a cab and I realise this really turns me on. You can't flag down anything in Yorkshire, other than a slapper. Watching Pete hail a cab is like something out of a Hollywood film, and we all know how much I like Hollywood. I am beginning to get that warm feeling in my belly again. We are dropped off right outside the bistro café. Surrounding us are designer children's wear shops, a jewelers (by appointment only) and a florist which makes the Chelsea Flower Show look like a poor relative.

The bistro is small but the spread of salads, sandwiches and cakes is unbelievable. Never have I seen so many colours in my life. My mouth is wet, as is my chin; I quickly wipe it on my sleeve. "Table for two," I ask the smiley gentleman behind the counter. He leads us to one very large white table where other people are sat. It's a sharing table. After my initial reluctance, I decide not to care. After all, this weekend is about Pete and I, no-one else matters. We are handed menus. I ask for the drinks menu. I am pointed to the small print at the bottom where it suggests ten different types of waters (or something like), the point being there is no alcohol. Just at the point where I am about to suggest we leave and go somewhere else, the couple next to us are brought their lunch. Wow. Okay, so they may not sell alcohol but we need to eat here. We have the most amazing lunch, we have a selection of three different types of salad – who knew a kumquat went so well with sprouting broccoli leaves and a pomegranate dew? I swear to try make this when I get home. It would, of course, have tasted even better if I had a large glass of pinot grigio to wash it down with, but that can be pudding, somewhere else. Pete is in heaven. He loves food and flavours. He wants to buy the grissini, at £10.50 a bag. Really? £10.50 for bread sticks? It's good, but that good?

I realise when we leave the bistro café that there aren't many cabs around here. In fact, there are none. There are a couple of Bentleys and Rolls Royces clearly

136

with drivers in, but none of these are waiting for us. We decide to walk a little further to see if there is a taxi rank around the corner. As we walk down the street, I discover a second hand children's clothing shop. How peculiar to have a charity shop in this neighbourhood. Although I want to pretend I don't shop at charity shops, we are in Notting Hill and I just know that the stuff in there is going to be good. I decide not to care and instead head straight in. Everywhere around us is Dior, Burberry, Tommy Hilfiger, Kickers, Doc Martins – oh my, I might have just wet my pants. Davina will look sensational in that Dior Hat, with the Ted Baker T-shirt, Armani skirt and those Kickers shoes. I gather it all up without checking the price. It's a charity shop, after all, what's the worst it will cost – £25.00? I take it to the counter, the assistant taps it into the till.

"That will be £347.00, please."

Fuck!

"Erm…"

Quick, I need an exit strategy.

"Oh, er, is that for age 5/6? Oh, silly me, I thought it was 15/16." She glares back at me. Of course it's not for a 15/16 year old, unless they are a midget.

"I'll, erm, have a look around for something else."

She's not impressed; she's giving me that sucking lemon look, which she does amazingly well without showing one line around her mouth – botox! I scour the shop and find Pete checking out a toy Bentley ride-in car. He's trying to work out where the engine goes. I whisper that we need to leave. A disappointed Pete exits the shop with me: the look of disappointment is written all over his face.

"Did you fart, Jess?" he asks, that being our usual reason for having to make a quick exit.

"No, I didn't fart. I daren't in there." I tell him about the clothing and my embarrassment at the checkout and we both giggle. We agree that Next and M&S are just as good for Davina. She doesn't need all that designer crap.

We decide to walk to Portabello Road, a bit more befitting of our price range. As we walk down the hill, we spot a couple sat in the window of a fabulous Italian café: the woman has a large glass of red wine and I decide we need a pit stop. Five minutes later, we are both sat in the other window seat and I'm lovingly caressing my large glass of Pinot Grigio. "My precious," I say, using my best Gollum voice. Pete is happy with his pint of something, I didn't pay much attention to what he ordered. After our second glass, I realise I should have ordered a bottle, it would have been a lot cheaper, but hey ho, now it's time to hit the shops.

As we walk down Portabello Road, everyone seems ultra-friendly. Some guy flirts with me a little as Pete and I are trying on hats from one of the stalls. In a strong cockney accent, he tells me that hat really suits me, apparently my face is perfect for it. *Such friendly people*, I think to myself. I decide to buy it. As I walk a little further down the road, I turn back and see the same guy telling the next lady that tries on a hat that she looks good too. Then it clicks that perhaps he is some kind of scout for that stall. All the same, I am pleased with my new hat.

My initial excitement at going into every antique shop starts to wane. Pete is starting to look a little bored, despite his promise to let me go in as many shops as I like, since I've done the museum and there won't be time for Oxford Street this time. However, I soon realise they are pretty much the same thing. One brass jug looks the same as the others and a real life stuffed deer head in our front room really won't go with our décor. I link arms with Pete and he gives me a kiss on the lips. This is the best day I've have had in years and I tell him that. Of course, I then instantly feel guilty because of course the best day ever should have been the day Davina came into this world, but the truth is, that was the worst day ever. Having some Indian doctor stick needles in my back and slit my stomach in half, after a full day of trying to push out an elephant through my vagina, does not rank in the 'best day ever' category.

Anyway, where were we? Ah yes, the best day ever – rephrase, the best day Pete and I have had together in a long time. That will suit the toffee-nosed, cake-making bitches. Having checked the time, we decide it's probably time to start heading back to the hotel to get ready. We want to grab a few cocktails at Covent Garden before dinner at The Vine. As we walk back up the hill, we come to a small crowd; there is music, 1940s style music, there are three fabulous girls dressed like army girls with bright red lipstick. I love that look – shame my teeth are slightly stained from all the coffee I drink (not red wine, I only drink that in winter). I ease my way through the crowd, grabbing Pete's arm to make sure he's with me. Those large Pinot Grigios are really kicking in now and I definitely feel like dancing. As the Chattanooga Choo Choo starts I feel my hips start to sway, then my left hand starts to click. Suddenly, I feel like Marilyn Monroe. I dance my way to the front; suddenly I am on my own, Pete hasn't joined me. As I beckon him over, he starts to retreat, he is withdrawing back into the crowd. Some guy joins me and the two of us start twirling about. The three girls are egging us on – this is ace. The crowd is clapping. This never happens up north. I take off my hat and start trying to do some kind of Fred Astaire jig with it. It lands in a puddle. Whatever, I can buy another. When the music stops, everyone claps. I clap at the girls, they clap back, I take a little bow, the random guy I have been dancing with kisses the back of my hand. For almost a whole twenty seconds I feel really special. When I turn to see if I can see Pete, I finally catch his gaze. He doesn't look impressed. In fact, he looks downright pissed off. I make a quick exit. I grab my now wet hat out of the puddle, because I'm not sure if I will be fined for littering, and make my way towards Pete.

"What's up?" I dare to ask.

"Why does it always have to be a show with you, Jess?"

"It's not a show," I say defensively. "It's called getting carried away with the moment. Having some fun, Pete. Are you embarrassed?"

"A bit."

"Oh, for fuck's sake, why?

Nobody knows us, who gives a crap?"

"I don't know why you couldn't have just watched it from the sidelines, why did you have to join in?"

"Because the moment took me, Pete. I want to have some fun, I need to have some fun. They enjoyed it, I enjoyed it, does it really matter what people think?" I can feel a small lump in the back of my throat building.

"I don't suppose it does. Sorry, it's just, you know, I don't like being the centre of attention."

"Yeah, well, I've discovered I do every now and again, and I need you to be my wingman, my Goose."

"Okay, sorry, let's not fall out."

Now, ordinarily I would remain pissed off for at least the next five hours, but since that would spoil a large part of the time we have left, I decide to let this one go. Pete hails a cab again but I'm not quite as excited this time. I'm still feeling a little sore. When we get in the cab, Pete pulls me to him. "Sorry," he says again, "I think I was just tired."

"It's okay," I say. I cuddle into him, all is forgiven.

When we get back to the hotel, I discover our luggage has already been delivered to our room. I eye it suspiciously, checking none of the locks have been tampered with. *Phew. All is secure.* I can now check out the room. It doesn't look anything like the room I booked online with Auntie Janet. It's much bigger, in fact. What's this? There is a sitting room. Pete is smiling. He's stood next to the coffee table. On the table is a champagne bucket with a bottle of champagne on ice and two glasses. Bless him. He's upgraded us. I throw my arms around his neck and plant a huge kiss on his lips. "Shall we?" he asks, gesturing to the champagne. Like he needs to ask. He pops open the champagne and pours my first. "Now then, let's get back to that snog." He puts his arms around my waist and pulls me to him. I can feel something is getting hard in his nether region.

"Wait," I say. "I've got a surprise for you too."

Ten minutes later after, breaking several locks, I grab the black carrier bag and disappear into the bathroom. After admiring the huge bath tub, which I swear I will try later, I start ripping the tags off the – what did they call it again? Peep Body, that's right.

"Jess, Jess, what are you doing in there?"

"Just a minute, can you top me up?" I hand out my empty champagne glass, exposing just my arm. "It'll be worth the wait, I promise." Okay, so the Peep Body is on, I try to stick on the nipple tassels but the left one keeps falling off. Bollocks. What can I use to make it stick? I look about the bathroom. Nothing. Wash bag. I check Pete's wash bag. Mr Sensible has everything in there. I unwrap the plaster and roll it around so the sticky side sticks to my nipple and the other to the tassel – perfect. Now, where's the cock rub cream and the vibrating butt plug – got them! I have a check in the mirror, I wet my fingers and ruffle up my hair. I then apply some cock red lipstick (Pete doesn't mind my coffee stained teeth). I'm ready.

"Music please," I shout from within the bathroom. Within a few seconds, Pink, *Just like a Pill*, is playing. Brill – I love Pink.

"You ready?" I ask.

"I've been ready for the past thirty minutes," shouts back a slightly exasperated Pete.

I step into the bedroom part of the suite. Pete is lying in his boxer shorts on the bed. "Tah dah," I say as I step out the bathroom, displaying my outfit with cock rub cream in the left hand and a vibrating butt plug in the other.

"Bollocks." Pete spits out his champagne over his chest.

"Don't you like it?" I ask, slightly sheepish.

"Like, I fucking love it, but what's that in your hands?"

"Ahh, you'll just have to wait and see."

I jump on the bed and the fumbling commences. Pete is inspecting every inch of my Peep Body. He's flicking the nipple tassels, which encourages me to try to shake them around. It's actually harder than you think to get a full circle. I place the cock cream and the vibrating butt plug on the side table, something to surprise him with later. Having explored every inch, Pete starts to warm me up. Luckily, this Peep Body has pop buttons for easy access to my nether region. After a good five minutes of foreplay, he lays on top of me and enters me. I'm enjoying this and am feeling almost ready to climax. A few strokes in and I decide it's time for Pete's surprise. I reach over and grab the vibrating butt plug. Without warning, I insert it right up his arse with one single thrust.

"FUCKING HELL."

His body shakes, he jerks, shudders, laughs and comes. His full weight is on top of me and the nipple tassels are now really digging in.

"Take it out," he shouts – actually, it's more of a scream. Urgh, I didn't expect I'd have to do that. I grab the cord at the base of the butt plug and yank it out. He jerks again and I feel something wet on my leg.

"Fucking hell, Jess, what did you stick up my arse?"

"Just this," I say, showing him the butt plug.

"A bit of warning wouldn't go amiss. Christ, I think I've burst a blood vessel." He's looking at his knob now, it does look slightly reddened.

"I just thought it would be a pleasant surprise."

"It was certainly a surprise," he replies. I'm not quite sure what to make of this, was it a good thing? I'm certainly not satisfied yet.

"I was just trying to spice things up, Pete," I say, slightly forlorn. He moves to my left and raises himself up onto on his elbow – his face is slightly flushed.

"A simple shag would have done to start with, you know, to get us warmed up, but I loved that you tried, I really do. Jess, don't cry." I can't help it. I'm not really sure why I am crying at this particular point, I can't decide if it's too much alcohol, the lack of orgasm or the fact that my nipples really hurt. I wipe the tears away.

"It's okay, I'm just, you know, disappointed. I wanted it to be really special."

"Trust me, it was definitely special. I won't forget that in a hurry. Look at you," he says, stroking my body. "What a fine specimen you are." This makes me smile.

This is the first time he has properly acknowledged all the effort I have made to get back into shape. He leans in and kisses me. I grab the back of his head. His hands are on my breasts, I reach for his cock "Ouch," he shouts, pulling away. He starts inspecting his knob again. "Sorry, but I think the old fella is in shock." I decide just to snuggle. Pete turns off the music and puts on the television. He instantly becomes entranced in whatever shite is on.

"I'm off for a bath," I say. He's not listening, he's switching between television and constantly inspecting his knob. He lays there naked, with what looks like a throbbing knob.

I get into the bathroom, run the bath and pour myself another glass of champagne. Whilst laying in the bath, I begin to re-think the past five minutes. I try to find the positives. It was good that I tried something different, exploring is great – okay, so I would perhaps have liked my nipple tassels playing with a bit longer and I was definitely in the market for an orgasm, but not to worry, there's always later. I lay back in the bath. As I begin to wash myself, I find the sponge is lingering between my legs slightly longer than needed and then he pops back into my head – Mr Bloom. Twenty five minutes later I emerge from the bathroom, cheeks slightly pink but with a smile on my face. Pete is asleep. I decide to wake him with the hairdryer as I begin to get ready for our night out.

Chapter Twelve
The Vine

If you don't frequent London regularly, you should be forgiven for being absolutely overwhelmed and excited by the number of bars and famous places you recognise. Of course, there is Buckingham Palace, but since I know for a fact they will never let me in there, it's not such a big deal, although the thought of Her Royal Highness sitting drinking sherry with a corgie on her lap whilst having her toe nails painted sends a slight shiver of excitement through me. As we go through Soho, I instantly recognise Stringfellows,

"Pete, look, Pete, look, it's Stringfellows."

I've always wanted to go there just to see if, on the off chance, Peter might be there himself and buy me a drink. When we are eventually dropped off in Covent Garden by the taxi driver, our bill is £45.00. Pete is mouthing at me, "What the fuck?" but we aren't going to challenge the bill, we enjoyed the tour. My excitement at seeing Stringfellows was worth it.

As I step out the taxi into Covent Garden, I am greeted by Shaun the Sheep. What the fuck is he doing here? This is a grown up weekend. I choose to ignore him. I link arms with Pete and we walk to the nice wine bar on the corner. Twenty minutes later, we walk out, feeling slightly perkier, although I'm sure Pete is walking with his legs slightly wider than usual. We head to the next bar and order two Margarita Madnesses. I always like the sound of a margarita but the taste is something quite difficult, it's fucking vile, actually, but I down it because they cost £10.00 each. It's some guy called Stephanuel's birthday in this bar. I know that because there are pictures of Stephanuel all over the bar. When some twenty year old girls saunter over to Pete on his way back from the toilet I decide it is time to leave. Pete suggests we stay and have another but I know if I have another of those margaritas I will pass out – maybe that was his plan?

We walk out of that bar straight into the next one, the American themed bar. I can't drink wine right now and I definitely know I cannot take another margarita so I order two mojitos – *surely they will sort me out, right?* Wrong. A few things I've learnt about mojitos: firstly, they don't make your breath smell minty fresh, secondly, with that amount of sugar on the outside of the glass you will need at least three fillings when you next visit the dentist, and thirdly, it's such an easy drink, you down the first couple in about sixty seconds flat. By the time we leave the American bar I'm pissed. Even Pete is wobbling. I know we are pissed because we are talking very loudly but keep shushing ourselves. As we approach The Vine, we try to sober up. I straighten my dress and re-apply my lipstick (blind). Pete puts his hands through his hair. We give each other the once over and give an approving nod. We are ready. There are men in suits on the door and I know if there is even a slight trip, we won't be allowed in. I have some experience in this.

We are through – phew. We are slightly early so are directed to the bar for a drink. The bartender hands us some menus and the drinks menu. Wow. The Vine must grow their own Pinot Grigio – at £85.00 a bottle, it must be a unique blend. Pete notices I am spending longer looking at the wine menu than the dinner menu. He takes a quick glance over my shoulder and orders the Pinot Grigio. He squeezes my leg and tells me to not worry about a thing, just enjoy. However, to compensate for the expensive wine and to prove I can be frugal when needed, I request a jug of tap water and ice. Surely The Vine's tap water is purified from their own springs?

After a good scour of the a la carte menu, I decide to order from the set menu. There isn't very much I fancy from the a la carte. I like the idea of sardines to start and roasted chicken breast followed by a cheese platter. When the waiter comes to take our order, I swear he looks disgruntled that we are ordering from the set menu. To try and appease him, I ask if there is a Menu of Discovery, but his response is sharp: "No, follow me." We are taken to the back of the restaurant. We walk past about thirty lovely looking booths but are placed close to the toilets in almost complete darkness. As we settle ourselves down, I accidentally take a seat on the gentleman's lap who is sat to the side. It's dark back here, I couldn't see very well and didn't notice there was another couple. After several apologies, I notice there are two other couples back here. I soon discover this is where the set menu orderers sit.

Once again, I decide not to let this bother me: this is our special weekend away. The drinks are brought over. By the time the starter arrives, I can barely focus. My sardine looks a little lost on the plate. He's stuck in the middle surrounded by some green looking dribble and I suddenly feel connected to him. I pick him up.

"Say hello to Norman," I say to Pete.

Pete laughs. He picks up his sardine. "Hi, I'm Bronwyn, hee hee."

The sardines are getting it on. The couple at the side, who still aren't amused about the sitting incident, are even less amused at us playing with our food. I don't care. I eat Norman and the green dribble. Food should be helping to sober me up but this stuff barely touches the sides. When my chicken breast with pureed celeriac arrives, I ask if there is a possibility of any chips on the side. "No," is the response. Pete's rabbit stew and dumplings seems to be hitting the spot. He looks like he is sobering up. I order a second bottle of Pinot Grigio because I've decided I am going to have a Big Mac on the way back to the hotel and that will sober me up. I know Pete will join me, he's always up for food. However, he's looking a little uncomfortable at my request for more wine. He leaves to use the bathroom – just as he goes, the next couple are brought to sit at the side of us. An older couple, very well to do; she is draped in jewels and I can tell his suit is not from M&S. I wonder what they are doing in the cheap seats. Then I realise, they've been squeezed in. They've obviously been somewhere else, a function of some sort, perhaps even cocktails at Buckingham Palace, this is their MacDonalds. The waiter fusses around them, apologising that these are the only seats they have at the minute but promising to move them once a booth becomes available – *bastard*. That's his tip gone down to 1%. I realise I've obviously been staring at the couple for slightly longer than socially acceptable. She smiles at me, I smile back. He smiles at me, I smile back. Then I find myself engaging in conversation with them.

"It's our anniversary," I lie. I just need an excuse to start a conversation and couldn't think of anything else to say.

"Oh, how lovely, congratulations," she replies.

"You look nice," I say. "Have you been to the theatre?"

"Oh no, dear, we've been at a drinks party at the House of Lords."

"Wow, House of Lords eh?" I'm nodding. I don't really know how to follow that. "We went to Portabello Road today, I bought a hat."

She smiles, he looks away. By this point, Pete has returned. He's looking from me to the other couple and gives a slightly awkward smile. I like talking to her, she's interesting, so I carry on the conversation.

"I love your necklace."

"Thank you, it's from my shop." She's opening up, I ask her where her shop is in case I've visited it, which of course I haven't since it is in Surrey and I've never been

150

to Surrey. She asks what I do and I tell her I am between jobs at the minute and how I wanted to spend the first five years with Davina as I will never get this time back, the fact she is now six and is at school full time has given me the opportunity to work on a couple of projects I have lined up. I don't disclose what they are because I haven't thought of what they are yet. Pete is chatting away with her husband. *This is nice*, I think to myself. Meeting new friends, in a fancy restaurant in London. I tell her, whose name is Catherine, that this is only the third time I have been to London, and how I love it so much. Catherine tells me she comes here at least once a month to shop whilst Robert attends to business in the City. I don't ask what 'business' he attends to because frankly I don't give a shit what he does, I just like my new friend, Catherine. I offer her some of our Pinto Grigio. She politely declines, she's quite happy with her Dom Perignon but, bless her, she tells the waiter to get another glass and pours me a glass of her fizz. Our conversation flows and I am beginning to feel really comfortable with Catherine. When my plate of cheese arrives, I barely touch it because I am so engrossed in my conversation with Catherine. I tell her a bit more about our day and my dancing. I don't mention the butt plug because, even as pissed as I am, there are limits. I tell her about the taxi ride in and passing Stringfellows Club. I swear her eyes light up at this point so I suggest we go, the four of us. Catherine seems up for it. Yay. I'm giddy. I look across at Pete, wondering if he heard. He heard all right. He is glaring at me, then Mr Catherine pipes up that he prefers the Spearmint Lounge. Whatever, I'm game.

"Jess, Jess," starts Pete. He leans in, probably wondering if we might need more cash if we are going to a strip club. "Stop it," he says.

"Stop what?" I ask, absolutely bewildered. I'm only making new friends, what's the problem?

"You are embarrassing me again," he retorts.

"Embarrassing you, again, what have I done now? I've not done anything."

"We aren't going to the Spearmint Lounge, okay?"

"Why not?"

"Pack it in, you know why not."

I am flummoxed, I don't understand. I stare across at Pete. He doesn't look happy, Catherine is looking across and I politely smile. I lean in and there is a bit of venom in my voice this time. "What is wrong with you? We are having a good time, all I said is about going to Stringfellows, he suggested The Spearmint Lounge. I just agreed. What harm can it do?"

"Can I have the bill?" Pete asks the waiter. In no less than thirty seconds it lands on the table with a homemade mint.

"Peter," I say, "I just want to have some fun. We don't have enough fun, everything is so serious and boring, why can't we just have a bit of fun?"

"Stop it," he snaps. I feel that lump building inside me again. However, this time instead of a lump it's a great big bloody mountain and the tears start to swell.

"I hate that you are embarrassed of me, you never used to be embarrassed of me, you know what I am like, you know what you married, why are you being like this? I just wanted to see some strippers," I protest. Pete is shifting around his chair, uncomfortable. Catherine and Mr Catherine are eating their starter, pretending to have a light conversation but deep down listening to the theatrics that are going on at our table. "I don't know you anymore, Peter, you've changed. I embarrass you, that's not my Pete, that's not the man I married." I'm proper sobbing now. The tears are running down my face, I cannot hide them. I don't care. It's like my world has come crashing down, the one person in my life who I thought I could have fun with and who would always accept me for being me has let me down. It breaks my heart. I tell him, "My heart is breaking, Peter." Pete is staring at me. After he taps in his pin number into the card machine, he immediately stands up.

"We are leaving."

I try to stand up. I knock over my Pinot Grigio. I say bye to Catherine, who looks at me with pity. I know my mascara will be somewhere near my chin. I say bye to Mr Catherine, who mumbles something back to me which sounds like chow. He too seems embarrassed.

When I hit the street everything starts spinning: the wine, the champagne, the cocktails, more wine, barely any food, I lean over the railings and throw up down the cellar of some offices. That'll be a nice surprise Monday morning. I chunder at least three times. It's in my hair.

"For fuck's sake, Jessica," Pete is furious. "Who's going to let us in a taxi now?" I can't speak. If I do I will probably be sick again. Pete grabs my arm and marches me towards the tube station. I want to protest but I've lost the ability to form any words. I just follow. I hold onto the railings in the underground to steady myself but Pete has his arm firmly around my waist, not in a loving, 'taking care of me' kind of way, but in a 'don't embarrass me by falling over' way.

When I step onto the tube it all seems a little surreal. I sit in the chair as directed by Pete and I slowly start to focus. Someone opposite is eating a Subway sandwich and it looks amazing. I start to feel a bit better. As I start to feel better the heat within me starts to burn. I shove Pete's arm off me. "Get off me," I snap.

"Shush," he tells me.

"Shush yourself," I respond, that being the best line I can come up with right now. "Why don't you go sit in the other carriage, that way I won't embarrass you, will I?" I edge to the side to look out the window. Bad idea, all I can see is darkness and shadows. I hate the tube. I think I'm going to be sick again. I will myself not to. Thankfully, there is nothing else to throw up.

When we get to our stop I stomp off the train, heading towards the exit. Pete is following me. "Jess, Jess, Jessica, slow down," he shouts. I am not slowing down, despite the fact I have no idea where I am or where I am going. He eventually catches up with me. He tries to grab my arm but I yank it away.

"I can't believe this, Peter. After all this time, I finally know exactly how you feel about me. Well, don't worry, I won't be embarrassing you anymore." I am choking on my tears. My performance now in the tube station is hitting Oscar territory, or so I believe. People are looking. I'm in a right state. Obviously, given the state I am in, it really does feel like my world has been turned upside down. When I arrive at the hotel, the concierge dares to ask if we've have had a good evening. Pete smiles. I sob some more. We get to our room, I get undressed and climb into bed, yanking the majority of the covers over me.

"Jess, can we talk?"

"Fuck you." That's all I wish to say on the matter. I sob some more for all the lovely things I did to make this weekend so special: the Peep Body, the butt plug – *ungrateful bastard.*

At 9.15 a.m. the phone rings. Wake up call. My head is banging. In fact, it's raging. I can barely open my eyes, they feel like golf balls. I head to the bathroom and drink about ten cups of water from the cold tap in the tooth brush holder. I start to remember the previous evening. I'm still upset. I'm perhaps not quite as upset as I was last night because, let's face it, going to a strip club with a couple old enough to be your parents is not really the done thing, but there was no need for Pete to behave the way he did. No, I'm not going to let him off the hook this easily. Whatever I may have said, done, or wherever I have vomited, he should have my back. Weren't they the vows we took when we got married?

155

Pete and I move about the hotel suite in silence. A few words are said, like, "Have you got everything? Are you ready? What time is the train again?" The hour and forty five minute train ride seems like forever. We sit in complete silence, neither of us wanting to speak to the other. I wonder if the whole thing has been blown out of proportion – was it really that big a deal? – but I still feel so upset. Something feels not right. I can't put my finger on it but there is a definite change between us. As the tears run down my face, this time I do my best to try and hide them. Something feels broken and I'm not sure how to fix it or if I even want it to be fixed.

Chapter Thirteen
It's Over

It's been a few weeks since London. Whilst Pete and I are talking again, it's more perfunctory talk, like what time he will be home, what we are having for dinner, etc. There has been no discussion about what happened that night, it's like it's been forgotten but it clearly hasn't, there is a huge elephant in the room but no-one wants to acknowledge it. We managed to be civil towards one another at Leigh and Jason's wedding. By the time the evening do started, I was completely shitfaced and don't remember a thing. I busy myself during the day as much as I can. I find I'm going to the gym almost every other day to do a class of some kind. I've ventured out from body pump and taken a few body combat classes. Since my fitness level has improved, I can actually jig about without falling into a heap on the floor. I particularly like the pretend boxing moves. I'm not sure who I am punching but Jade stands well back. One day when I leave after a particularly sweaty combat session, I pass an advertisement on the notice board: 'Wanted, receptionist, three days a week, flexible hours.' Since I spend so much time here anyway, I decide I might as well apply. I'm on first name terms with the most of the staff here now so when I express an interest, fifty minutes later, I walk out of the Charles Frogman Club as their newly appointed receptionist.

When I get home, I feel a little brighter. I have something to look forward. When I collect Davina from school she instantly asks what is wrong with me. I'm confused. "You are smiling, Mummy."

When we get home, I start to make tea. I'm a bit excited to share my news with Pete when he gets home. Just as I start to make the cheese sauce to go with the lasagna, I get a text from Pete. 'Eat without me. Will be home late. P.' Oh. Okay. Well, I will just have to tell him later. Davina walks into the kitchen.

"What's that, Mummy?"

"Cheese sauce, darling, for the lasagna."

"I don't like cheese sauce."

"Yes you do, darling, you've had it lots of times."

"I don't like that yukky yellow stuff," she says, grabbing the wooden spoon and ramming it into the mixture. Ordinarily, I would have blown by now but I'm slightly upbeat so I let it pass.

"Well, sweetheart, this is what we are having, you will like it when's it's finished, I promise."

"I DON'T LIKE IT," she shouts. "I'M NOT EATING IT." I am starting to feel irritated, which shouldn't be happening when I was feeling so upbeat.

"Davina, this is tea. It's this or toast."

"I HATE TOAST," she shouts, "I HATE YOU. I WANT DADDY."

"Yes, well, Daddy isn't going to be home until late tonight, so tough," I snap back. My good mood is evaporating. She sticks her tongue out and makes to leave. I grab her arm. "Don't you dare, young lady, I'm your mummy. Don't you dare stick your tongue out at me, you spoilt little brat." Ouch, I didn't mean for it to come out like that but it did. I hold my breath, not knowing quite what to expect. Davina calmly turns to me. She displays her elbow.

"Talk to the elbow cause it ain't worth the extension," she says as she lowers her arm in my direction. She saunters back off into the lounge, which is probably a good thing because I'm eyeing the carving knife right now. OMG, if ever spoke to my parents like this, my ear would have been red raw and I wouldn't have been able to sit down for a week.

I wait for Pete, I am excited to tell him about my new job. Okay, so it's hardly a career but, for now, it suits. It's not like I couldn't go back into marketing if I wanted to. I'm sure there are plenty of companies out there wanting a marketing whizz like me, I just can't give that kind of job my full commitment at this time. I mean, I've not chosen the reception job because I am fearful no-one will actually want me, that's just ridiculous.

When it gets to 10.30 p.m., I begin to feel a little anxious. Okay, so things haven't been great between Pete and I since London, but he is coming home, right? I mean, he wouldn't leave me standing, knowing I've got some news. Oh, but right, he doesn't know that part yet. At 11.30 p.m., I am truly pissed off. He hasn't telephoned or anything. He is clearly still punishing me for London – bastard. Well, fine, gloves are off. *I'm off to bed*, I tell

myself. *I'm not waiting up for this prick another minute.*
I put the dregs of the Pinot Grigio into the fridge and head
to bed, expecting to fall into a deep sleep. It's 12.30 a.m.
I'm still wide awake. I hear a car on the drive, the door
closes and then I hear the front door being unlocked.
Since our bedroom is above the kitchen, I can hear
everything. I can hear the scraping of my lasagna into a
bowl, next comes the dial on the microwave. Bastard, I
wish I hadn't left him any now. Even if he did ring to say
eat without him, he should have called to say he would
be this late.

I must have eventually fallen asleep because when I
wake up, it's 07.45, which is strange. I usually have a
wake up call from Davina around 06.15 a.m. I check the
other side of the bed; the pillow is dented but there is no
Pete. As I sit up, I hear the television on downstairs. The
faint sound of "Mishka, mushka, Mickey Mouse," tells
me Davina is awake and watching television. I head
downstairs. When I walk into the lounge, Davina is
dressed in her school uniform, the uniform I ironed
yesterday. Well, okay, maybe not ironed, hung out on the
washing line and then glided my hands up and down her
top and bottoms to smooth out the wrinkles, but that
counts, right? She looks really smart, someone else has
ironed her uniform for her. Pete. Pete must have done this
last night. Why? Guilt, I decide. He didn't make Davina's
bedtime, which is not unusual, but this time, he didn't
even make a call before bedtime. That's why he ironed
her uniform, to ease his guilt.

"How long you been up, sugar?" I ask.

"I don't know, Mummy but Daddy came in to see me and I woke up. He got me dressed and gave me some breakfast."

I'm starting to feel tense.

"Where is he now, darling?"

"He said he had to go to work, he made me scrambled eggs on toast."

"Did he now?" I ask with a little venom in my voice. "Why didn't he wake me, sweetheart?"

"Daddy said not to wake Mummy or she will be cross. He said if I'm a good girl and just watch television we will go swimming at the weekend."

"Did he now?" I find myself repeating. *Well, I'm just bloody redundant aren't I?* Super dad, who misses bedtime, arrives home at silly o'clock but finds time to iron a uniform, make scrambled egg and sneak out all before I get up. Well, I'll just, just… have a shower this morning. Perhaps for once I will look presentable on the school playground.

After dropping off Davina at school, Carlton and I decide to go for a coffee at Westwells Garden Centre. It is, of course, full of pensioners – in fact, two coaches pulled in as we arrived – but we managed to beat the queue. Carlton only had to shout that there was a three for two offer on shortbread at the recently opened Edinburgh Wool Mill section of the garden centre and there was a mass exodus. I won't feel sorry for the lady serving behind the counter at the Edinburgh Woollen Mill, she knew what she was signing up for when she took the job.

Carlton and I walk to the table. Carlton kindly offers to carry the tray with his fennel tea and my hot chocolate and cheese scone. I can't resist them when they look like a small child has blown yellow snot all around the base, so cheesy.

"Out with it, then, what's bothering you?" he asks.

Erm excuse me, but how, why, does, you don't know me well enough to know there is a fundamental problem in my life right now.

"Honey, you've been presentable at the school playground recently, even your hair has been brushed. Normally, you look like something a cat dragged through a hedge backwards. I told Joffrey I thought there was something up with you."

"It's nothing really," I find myself confiding. "Pete and I are just going through a, you know, rough patch."

"Oh, but what about your London trip, I thought that was a romantic weekend away?"

"It was," I reply. "Well, for the first few hours we got on great, but it all went a bit pear shaped after that, and we kinda haven't really spoken since."

"Since? But wasn't that five weeks ago?" Carlton has reached out and grabbed my arm now. I can see pity and concern on his face.

"It's no biggy, we'll get through it." I smile back at him. "Anyway, did I tell you I start a new job tomorrow?" I ask, changing the subject. He clearly doesn't believe a word of it but he certainly knows me well enough to know the subject is closed, for now anyway. At this point, two old ladies walk over to us.

"Ethel, look, it's Carlton."

"Morning, ladies," says Carlton, slightly camper than usual. "Looking gorgeous as ever, I see."

"Ooh, you cheeky young man. Isn't he cheeky, Ethel?" Ethel is too busy staring at me.

"Oh, I'm sorry, love, are we interrupting? Come on, Florence, these two are in the middle of something."

As they start to walk away, Florence turns to Ethel. "Did you see that, I always thought he batted for the other team, you know, a turd burglar." Carlton and I laugh. He removes his hand from my arm; he clearly doesn't want word getting out he's changed sides. It could destroy his business.

We sit for a little longer, finishing our drinks, and I smudge as much of the remaining butter I can get onto the last crumb of cheese scone.

"Come on, I can squeeze you in before my next appointment," says Carlton.

"Squeeze what?" I asked, perplexed.

"I can do your hair, ready for your new job. Come on, sweetie: new job, new look, new you."

I ponder this for about a millisecond, I am in.

Two hours later, I emerge from Carlton's house. I'm a whole new woman. Well, okay, not quite, but I have a trendy inverted bob and I'm no longer a mousey-coloured brown, but raven. I'm chuffed as punch. I like this look. It's less mumsy and more MILF.

When I collect Davina from school, she completely ignores me. She stays at Mrs Crecher's side. I am waving like a lunatic from the side lines but she doesn't see me.

Some of the other mothers are looking across at me and I can see it on their faces. Okay, so I may have gone slightly over the top, having changed my jeans for my tight PVC black trousers with a see through blouse. Well, it's not completely see through, you can only make out the shape of my bra. The full face of make-up perhaps wasn't needed but I need to get a feel for how my new look was going to work out, ready for work tomorrow. I can hear the whispering but I don't actually give a shit. I'm enjoying the attention: negative attention is better than no attention, right?

I eventually walk up to Mrs Crecher. Davina recognises me. "Mummy, what have you done?"

"I've had a makeover, darling," I say, smiling. "Do you like it?"

"No! I hate it, I want my old mummy." I smile. I can't scream at her in front of Mrs Crecher. I can tell she is waiting for just one more reason to call social services as it is.

"Oh don't worry, sweetheart, it's still me." It's at this point I decide to drop into the conversation that I will now be working a couple of days a week. "Just so you know, I start work tomorrow. It's just three days a week in school hours, at my gym, but, you know, just in case I should get stuck in traffic or something, I will be on my way." Mrs Crecher looks me up and down.

"If you are late, Davina will be placed in the detention hall with the other children. The end of the school day is a busy time and I cannot be childminding. I suggest you ensure you leave in good time." *Bitch.* Davina looks up at me.

"I don't want to go in the detention, Mummy. What's detention?" She looks worried.

"Don't worry, sweetheart, Mummy will be here to collect you from school. I mentally stick two fingers up at Mrs Crecher as we leave the playground. She's not getting an end of term leaving present this year.

When Pete gets home later that night, I make sure I am still looking my best. I keep checking my hair in the mirror, well, actually, I'm just loving my new look and keep checking myself out. I am stood by the sink when he walks through the door. He is on his phone. He barely glances at me. I loiter around him like a lost puppy waiting for acknowledgment.

"I'll get onto it first thing. Yes, I will double check them tonight. Bye." He hangs up.

"Hi," I say, a little too upbeat.

"Hi, we got any beer?" He still hasn't made eye contact.

"Yes, let me."

I open the fridge, pop off the lid and hand him a Bud. He is tapping into his phone. He tries to take the beer from my hand but I won't let go. He looks up. Finally, I have his attention.

"You've done something different," he says, in a noncommittal way.

"Yes, it's my new look, ready for my new…" His phone rings.

"Brian, hi, yes the outlook configuration has…" He walks out the kitchen. Just as he leaves, he turns around and mouths, "It's nice." *Nice. Nice, eh?* Isn't that what old people say for a cup of tea? 'How's about a nice cup of tea?' *Prick.* Screw him. The evening goes by with barely any conversation. Pete spends most of the evening either on his telephone or tapping into his laptop. I give Davina a bath and read her a bedtime story, spending longer than usual. It's normally a quick Gruffalo story but tonight, I opt for Peter Rabbit – three chapters of Peter Rabbit, actually. Davina is, of course, asleep, but I carry on reading them anyway; they are a comfort. After that, I head to bed to read my book, the same one I've been reading for the past five years.

When I wake up the next morning, Pete has already left. How does he do that? Am I sleeping deeper again now? I had presumed that the days of deep sleep had gone after having Davina. I had lost the ability to completely shut down, I would hear a pin drop. Any little noise could keep me awake for hours. Oh well, at least I don't have to engage in any conversation. It's my first day at Charles Frogman. I'm nervous but excited. Thankfully, my hair has remained intact and so it needs little work this morning, which isn't surprising given the amount of hairspray Carlton used. I had to feel my way out of his house yesterday because of all the spray.

After dropping Davina at school, I head to the gym. I have my sports kit in the boot, as they said I could do any classes I like during my break. My induction with the office manager, Stephanie, takes up the morning, going through the boring bits like health and safety etc. I am then given the official tour, not the one you get as a member but the one non-members get to see, like the kitchen, the staff room, the lockers. There is a chill out lounge for staff only. When I go in, Jade is sat there doing some kind of yoga meditation type stretch on the matt. She smiles but is too engrossed in her 'thing' to engage in conversation. As Steph and I turn to leave, I come face to face with Adonis. I feel like one of those cartoon characters whose tongue droops from their mouth and lands on the floor. Before me is a 6ft5 hunk of a man. His chest pokes out about 5ft from his rib cage, his biceps are perfectly toned and his thighs look like they could crush my entire body, I shudder at the thought. Steph has gone all gooey-eyed.

"Erm, and this is Frankie, our newest member of the PT Team."

"Hi," says Frankie. He has a squeakier voice than I imagined, slightly effeminate. I expected to him have a gruff voice, but I can forgive it. Then he truly would be the world's perfect specimen of a man. Steph is sweating. I'm always amazed how many of the office staff at the gym are overweight, unfit women. I wonder if they misread the instructions and think that just working in a gym helps you lose weight. It's either that or they just enjoy all the eye candy, men and women.

I spend the afternoon with the other receptionist, Leah. She is clearly a breed of her own kind of stupid. She shows me how to answer the telephone. Wow. I've only been doing it for the past thirty five years, I'm so glad for the various demonstrations.

"So, this is how we answer. Good afternoon, Charles Frogman, how may I help you?"

Got it.

"And this is how we direct a call: 'Good afternoon, Charles Frogman, how may I help you? Directing you to the office, directing you to the gym, directing you to the crèche'." Directing you to my arse! To be fair, I appreciated the rundown on the computer booking system. Technology has never been my strong point. By 2.30 p.m. I am up and running. I have answered my first phone call for the taxi rank, wrong number. At three p.m., I clock off. Whilst it isn't the most stimulating job, it has been good to do something different. It has also been good to see how many people I know who just come in and sit and drink coffee and do bugger all. They pretend they are taking some kind of business call on their way in but, seriously, you are fooling no-one. I never do that – if I am gym-bound it's always to do some kind of fitness regime. I never think I will just pop in for a cuppa, I couldn't cope with the guilt. The fact I am now working here doesn't count.

I manage to pick up Davina on time. I could see the look of relief on her face when she saw me arrive. When I got the finger from Mrs Crecher I assumed it was to see how my first day had gone… wrong!

"Davina has wet her pants today."

"Right, okay." *What does she want me to say?*

"It was anxiety." *Thank you, Dr Crecher but it was probably just the fact she got caught short.* I turn to my daughter.

"Did you forget you needed a wee?"

"No."

Oh.

"Well, what happened, sweetheart?"

"I was anchous, Mummy." Mrs Crecher lets out a small smile at the side of her mouth. I hate this bitch.

"What were you anxious about, darling?"

"That I would have to go to the hole of defention." Mrs Crecher looks more smug.

"Well, I'm here, darling, no need to worry." I protectively put my arm around my daughter and lead her away from the Crecher.

Just as we hit the school gate, Carlton comes running through. There is panic on his face.

"What's up?" I ask.

"Jesus, I'm late. I'm never late, but Ethel's blue rinse went wrong and we had to do it again. Have you seen Lionel?"

"Yes, he was with Mrs Crecher."

"Bollocks," says Carlton. I put my hands over Davina's ears.

"She's on the warpath, hun, run for it."

"Oh Christ." Carlton dashes off through the playground, ducking and diving past the hordes of children. He runs like a girl. Poor Carlton, if he doesn't get there in time you can guarantee Lionel will have a meltdown in the Hall of Detention. Poor kid. Poor Carlton.

The rest of the week goes by in a breeze. Whilst my new job may not be stimulating to the mind, it's good to get up each morning for something purposeful, other than the school run, of course. I'm finding I am enjoying the simplicity of my job. Most people at the gym are really friendly. For example, the tennis coach, Keith, is very friendly. He stands and chats away every opportunity he gets. He has a huge sack of balls with him and always wears shorts no matter the weather. I like working here. It's a bit like a family. Just before I left on Friday, I managed to catch a glimpse of PT Frankie in action. All his clients are women (I checked his client list), most of them don't need a PT, they actually just need to eat a kebab and stay out of the sun. He has quite a following. He smiled at me when he saw me looking. I guess it happens quite a lot. I wasn't embarrassed. I'm staff, after all.

Of course, Pete still has no idea about my job. His ear has been permanently attached to his phone. When we did actually sit down together the other night I decided I wasn't going to tell him. I don't really know why I wouldn't tell him, I suppose I wanted to see if he asked, but of course he wouldn't ask because he doesn't know I have a job, but still, I wanted him to ask. (Ladies – you get it!)

On Friday, Davina and I make homemade pizza. I treat myself to a large glass of Pinot Grigio at four p.m.

because I have been working this week. Somewhat unusually, I allow Davina to take over the reins of decorating the pizza. I am far too busy checking Facebook to see what has been happening in the world. When I finally lift my head from my iPad, the bottle of Pinot Grigio has been devoured and the pizza looks like something you get from one of those plates filled with rock that look like food from the seaside sweet shops you get in Scarborough. There is tomato, peppers, olives (all of which I cut beforehand, I should add), followed by M&M's, Maltesers, gherkins, a packet of Jelly Tots and a load of grated mozzarella. Hmm. Take out, maybe? Although I am quite curious to see what Jelly Tots look like when cooked.

When Pete gets home, I am scraping out a black plate of tar from the oven. Someone forgot it was in there. Perhaps if I hadn't given Davina that giant pack of Cheesy Doritos to munch on whilst I cooked the pizza, she would have remembered she was hungry and come and disturbed me. However, I got a bit carried away with Facebook. I have so much to share this week and comment on. Had I known it would take this long I definitely would have opted for take-out pizza.

"What's that?" asks an apparently starving Pete.

"Dinner," I reply. I can tell he is waiting to see if I am joking. "It went a bit wrong. Apparently Jelly Tots don't work well on pizza."

He doesn't look amused, and there it is. I can see it in his eyes. That look of 'well, what have you been doing all day?' *Go on, just say it, just say it*, I say to myself. I

171

am goading him now, I think my head is cocked to one side.

"What's wrong with you?" he asks.

"I'm tired, actually."

"Oh."

Chuffing 'oh'.

He digs into the crisp cupboard and starts munching on the Cool flavour Doritos. "Aren't you going to ask?" I'm still goading.

"Ask what?"

"Why I'm tired." I am becoming increasingly fucked off. I think he's getting the message.

"Why are you tired?" he asks with a 'woe is you' expression.

"Well, I have had a busy week at work, actually."

"What's wrong with Davina?" asks Pete. He's clever enough to not suggest I don't work, even though he doesn't know I actually now have a proper job, other than Davina.

"Well, actually…" I start. His head is back in the cupboard. "I'm now working at the —"

"Jess, why the fuck are there twenty cans of sweetcorn in the cupboard?"

"Oh," I laugh, "I got the order wrong on the online shop. I meant to press two but pressed twenty."

"Well why didn't you send them back?"

"Well, I guess I thought we would eat them, it's not like they will go out of date any time soon." (They will remain in there with the other cans we've had since 1998.)

"Jeez, it's not rocket science, you know? I don't even know why you have to order online, it's not like you haven't got plenty of time on your hands."

Oh, you bastard. Here it is, this is what I have been waiting for. An eruption from him, I knew it's been brewing. I glare.

"What do you mean, Peter, are you suggesting I don't pull my weight?"

"Well, to be honest, Jess, all you seem to do is go to the gym, drink Pinot Grigio and spend all my cash."

"Is that really all you think I do? What about caring for our daughter, keeping the house tidy, making your tea, does none of that count?"

"I don't call switching the television on and off and dropping and collecting her at and from school really counts. I'm the one who irons her uniform, you just leave it hanging. As for tea, yeah, well, it looks really appetising."

I am cut, I think I'm bleeding from the head. I cannot get my head straight to take all of this in.

"It sounds to me, Peter, like you don't really like living here that much anymore."

"Is that how it sounds?" he asks with a degree of sarcasm.

"You know what, I'm not sure I like living with you anymore either. You've turned into a middle aged bore. You are about as much fun as a fart in a thunder storm."

"Just because I don't get shitfaced every night doesn't make me less fun, Jess."

Ouch. The gloves are off. I stare.

"Well, if I am such a bad wife and mother, why don't you fuck off and leave us?"

"Fine."

"Fine," I reply.

Pete grabs his laptop, his phone and his keys and leaves, slamming the kitchen door behind him. I quickly run and lock the door, leaving the keys in it to make sure he cannot get back in. I am shaking.

"Daddy, Daddy, where's Daddy gone?"

Bollocks.

"Daddy has had to go back out, darling."

Davina runs to the window and catches Pete's car leaving the driveway.

"Daddy!" she shouts. "You made Daddy leave, you shouted at Daddy."

Oh crap, she heard.

"Listen," I say, bending down to her level. "Sometimes, grownups fall out. It's okay, it's not your fault." Davina's bottom lip is quivering.

"I want my daddy."

She runs off into the lounge. I can't cope with this right now. I need a minute. *What just happened, did he really just leave, is that it? Is it the end? Is our marriage over because I bought twenty cans of sweetcorn?* I cannot get my head around this. I need a friend. I text Faye. "Hi, hun, are you free for a chat? I think Pete and I have split up." Two minutes later, I get a text back, she's coming around after the kids have gone to bed.

By the time Faye gets here, I've managed to get Davina to bed and asleep. The promise of pancakes in the morning and a trip to Toys R Us tomorrow is all that was needed. It's times like this I am grateful my child can easily be bought. I'm three quarters of the way through my second bottle of Pinot Grigio, listening to Ben Howard, Old Pine. When Faye walks in, she immediately asks if there has been a power cut. I forgot to turn on the lights in the lounge. I cannot answer, the sobbing begins and it's proper sobbing, there is snot and everything. Faye rings Ian and tells him she won't be back tonight. She can't leave me, especially after I switch to Joni Mitchell.

The next morning I feel broken, everything hurts, particularly my chest. I know my head hurts from the three bottles of Pinot Grigio I consumed last night but the pain is not a hangover. I cannot remember getting to bed but somehow I am in my nightie. Davina. I quickly check the clock, it's 9.05. *Crap.* I rush to her bedroom; she's not there. I go downstairs, she's colouring with Faye. Davina runs up to me and gives me a cuddle. Where did this come from?

"Oh and a kiss," she says. She kisses me on the cheek then looks to Faye as if to say, 'that's all I had to do, right?' I can feel the tears well again. I leave and go into the kitchen. I check my phone. There is a message from Pete at 01.43, 'I've checked into the Belmont, I'll stay here until I can find somewhere else. I'll be back to pick some stuff up later and to sort out seeing D. Pete.' I throw the phone into the sink. Faye comes into the kitchen. I point to the phone. She picks it up and reads the message from Pete.

"See, I told you," I say. "It's for real, he really has left me over sweetcorn." Faye looks puzzled.

"This is just so not Pete, Jess. He adores you and Davina, I'm sure he will be back, probably with his tail between his legs." I don't believe her, I know this is it. I can feel it in the pit of my stomach. I just can't believe it has ended over sweetcorn, thank fuck he never saw the eighteen bottles of Sancerre I wrongly ordered. I'm going to need those now, although I'm not sure I will ever be able to eat sweetcorn again.

Chapter Fourteen
What now?

Pete turned up later on the Saturday after Faye left. Bless her, she made me coffee, ran me a bath, put my bed sheets in the wash, made Davina's pancakes and drew out various characters for her to colour. When Pete arrived, I have to say, he looked pretty shit too, which gave me some satisfaction. However, he was cold towards me, but then I guess I was towards him. I had kindly pulled out some of his belongings and thrown them in a bag so he didn't need to hang about. I shoved in the knitted jumper his mother made for him which he always refused to get rid of but would never wear. It took up almost a whole shelf in the wardrobe.

What made it really hard was watching Davina's face when she saw him. She lit the room up, she was beaming from ear to ear. Notice how kids always smile for their dads like that and never you? Going with the majority here, most stay at home parents are mums. We do everything for our little darlings, all the practical stuff, but they never give us the same smile they have for their fathers. Just because they have time to push them on the swing, throw them in the air and are generally better at making up fake voices for stories, doesn't mean they are any better a parent. Who is the constant, consistent, loyal, hardworking, devoted, loving, cake-making, tea-making, bathing, always there no matter what parent? As Davina runs into Pete's arms I see the tears in his eyes. This is heartbreaking. He should just apologise and we can get through this. Perhaps we need some therapy. I stand there with glistening eyes, willing him to apologise, but he doesn't make eye contact with me.

"I've packed some stuff for you," I goad. He puts Davina down. She glares at me.

"Where is Daddy going, Mummy?" Pete bends down to her level.

"Daddy has to stay away for a while, darling."

"But you promised to take me swimming this weekend." She looks at him with a frown. *Ha! Get out of that one, scumbag.*

"Well, perhaps if Mummy says it's okay, we can go tomorrow." *Oh, great, make it all my decision.* How can I say no? I nod. It's all I can do. If I try and speak I will blurt out a rather dramatic "fine," and burst into tears.

"Yay for Daddy," says my easily bought six-year-old. I wonder if there is any way I can make her say how much she likes sweetcorn, to prove a point, but I just can't think of a way of getting that message through without it sounding deliberate. As Davina runs back into the lounge, Pete starts grabbing some items out of the fridge into a carrier bag. I watch with interest to see what he is taking. He grabs some beer, his precious coffee beans and some cans of Red Bull. Is that it? He doesn't go anywhere near the tinned jar cupboard; it's as if it will burn him if he touches the handle. I'm still stood there. I don't know what to do. What do you do in this sort of situation? Normally, when he is going away I check he has the vitals: toothbrush, toothpaste, shaving cream, clean boxers, the usual. Now that he's leaving us, gulp, what am I to suggest he takes? Washing up liquid, Persil, toilet paper, spatula, DVDs, books like 'How to mend your wife's breaking heart' or 'How to be a better husband'. Pete doesn't check the bag. I don't know why, perhaps he finds this hard too. You wouldn't think he does to look at him, but then blokes are better at hiding their feelings.

"Right," he says. "I'll be back to pick up Davina at eleven." Oh, great, a fucking lie in then. I don't say it but think it.

"Whatever," I say.

He leaves. So that's it then. Ten years of marriage down the pan. *Christ, just wait until his mother finds out.* I shudder at the thought. I know if I tell my family they won't be surprised. It's normal in my family to go through a few marriages before you meet Mr Right, except for Auntie Janet. Auntie Janet will be disappointed. She always thought, like me, Pete was my Mr Right. Oh Christ, I'm sobbing again.

Somehow, the days pass by. The hardest is definitely the weekends. Now that I am working Monday, Wednesday and Friday and at the gym exercising Tuesday and Thursdays, the weeks go by much quicker. The fact I am spending five days a week at the gym is not a concern, I'm working, earning and exercising, and what's more, it's a distraction from my life right now. God knows what I would do if I didn't have this. Pete and

I have agreed via text message that he can see Davina pretty much as often he wants/can but as a starting point, we agree he will collect her from school each Tuesday and spend Saturdays and Sundays with her every alternate week. If he can get away any earlier in the week, he can have her too. I'm not going to stop her seeing her dad. She loves him and should see him as often as possible. To stop it is punishing the child and that in my opinion is definitely a reason to call Social Services.

At present, Pete doesn't have her overnight. I know he doesn't want her to see he is living in a double room in a hotel. At age six, Davina wouldn't understand. It's been three weeks since Pete left and we have barely spoken. Everything is done via text message. When he returns Davina, I hand him his post. When he dropped her off on Tuesday, he noticed my work badge. This struck up our first conversation in weeks.

"You're working at Charles Frogman now?"

"I've been working there for the past four weeks," I reply. I can see he is doing the math. His face looks a little pain stricken, unless it's my imagination. I stand, waiting. I'm not sure what I'm waiting for, perhaps just a 'Well done, Jess,' or a nod of approval. Nothing. He turns and leaves. Fuck him.

I didn't sleep well that night. Something was troubling me but I am not sure what. The next morning, I had to put on an extra layer of make-up to cover the bags. Of course, I'm now well-adjusted to getting up earlier than Davina to get ready for work. Somehow I have moved from the conscious incompetent parent to the conscious competent parent. When I drop her at the playground, I am received a little warmer by the toffee-nosed cake-making bitches. The chavs, of course, hate me, I daren't make eye contact for fear of being lynched. Carlton always looks at me with those pity eyes: "How you holding up, sweetie?" Carlton is really beginning to grate on my tits. Does he need to ask, can't he see I am fine? My hair is done, my make-up is on, I'm only late about once a week which is better than before, when it was usually at least twice, or maybe thrice, but who's counting – oh, the Crecher, that's right. I've had to get it together; my husband has left me over twenty cans of sweetcorn. I had to get my shit together.

When I arrive at work later that day, it's not a good start. Leah is off sick – laryngitis, apparently. I'm not surprised. Why use one word when a thousand will do? It had to catch up with her at some point. However, today is particularly busy. It's the penultimate week before the kids break up for summer. Everyone has decided to try and get fit two weeks before their holiday. Even Stephanie has started hitting the gym in her lunch break. However, sitting on the rowing machine and watching Sky News really doesn't help shift the pounds.

It's manic. For some reason, today everyone forgot to bring their membership cards so I have to ID them on the screen to let them in. Next comes the barrage of kid's clubs bookings. All the carrot eating stiffs want to get their children booked into every activity going. By noon I am knackered, and I've only been here for a couple of hours. But then it happens, Kitty Vanderlosse saunters up to the reception desk. She must be about sixty five, I reckon. She is always wearing a tennis dress and has the fittest legs I have ever seen. I can tell she's definitely older because her skin is sagging a bit, the Caribbean tan she wears and always has topped up shows this. She arrived earlier, she never smiles, she just smacks her card against the barrier and she is through. This time she is walking from the inside of the club and there is determination in each step.

"Excuse me, excuse me?" I look at her but she looks unfriendly. I turn to see if anyone is behind me. "Yes, you, why is my court booked out?"

"I don't know," I calmly respond. "Shall I take a look for you?"

"Well, it's better than just standing there doing nothing."

I wasn't doing nothing, how rude – I was playing Candy Crush. I check the computer. "Which court do you think you booked?"

"I don't THINK I booked anything. I BOOKED court 10, between twelve and one, and there is someone else on my court."

I tap some more into the computer, I always wanted to do my David Walliams impersonation, 'computer says no.'

"I'm sorry, Ms Vanderlosse, but there is no booking for you today." By this point, Kitty is joined by her fellow tennis-goers, Margery Sinclair, Trixie Beauxer and Denise Dordogne; they sound like they should be running in the Grand National.

"It's VanderloZZe, pronounced with a z, and I booked the court myself on Monday, on the line."

I can't help but smirk, 'on the line'.

"Online you mean?" I ask, I can't resist.

"Yes, on the line, like I said."

"I'm sorry, but that court is booked out already to another member and I cannot see you've made any bookings for this week." Kitty is starting to look purple. She walks directly up to the reception desk with her tennis racket held like she is about to use my head as her tennis ball.

"Listen, I'm not some halfwit who works behind a desk all day, I've run eight businesses in my time so I think I know if I have booked a court or not. Now, you better find me a court, or is that too difficult for you to understand?"

Now ordinarily, I wouldn't have taken this, I would have rose up to this wrinkled looking bitch and given her a good dressing down but, at the minute, I'm feeling vulnerable. My marriage ended over twenty tins of sweetcorn, I cannot face losing my job over a tennis court. Something inside is starting to happen, my eyes are starting to get wet. *Oh shit, no, don't let this happen. Anything but this.* This wanton trollop does not deserve my tears.

"Is there a problem, do you not understand, parlez-vous anglais?"

At this point Steph has appeared from the back office.

"Everything okay?" Steph asks.

I cannot control it, I get up and make a run for it. *Horrid, nasty bitch, there was no need for that, I was only trying to help.* I can't stop the sobbing and it's the kind of sobbing where you can't catch your breath. I can feel I am going bright red. I run through the gym and into the staff lounge. Luckily no-one is in there. I collapse in a heap and sob my heart out. Since I have the cushion stuffed over my head, I don't hear when the door opens. The only thing I notice is when a hand touches my back. "Are you okay?" asks a peculiar squeaky voice. I look, expecting to see Mickey Mouse, but it's Frankie.

Oh crap. I must look a right state.

"I'm fine," I manage to say back through the sobs.

"You don't look fine, here." He hands me some tissues. As I blow my nose I feel the snot leak either side of the tissue. I can taste some in my mouth. *Oh, fuck.* Frankie is sat down next to me now with his large bicep-popping arm on my shoulder.

"Have you had bad news?" he asks.

Great, thanks for that, Frankie, yes, bad news will explain this state.

"Yes, very bad."

"I'm sorry, I lost my cat last year and I was in bits. Was it a loved one?"

"Erm, yes, my, erm, my Auntie Janet has died."

"Oh, that's terrible. I'm so sorry. Here." He pulls me into his chest and gives me a full on bear hug. Oh boy does that feel nice. He smells of a mixture of sweat and coconut oil. My nose is crushed on his hard pecs. I'm starting to frame myself a little. Why the fuck did I choose Auntie Janet? What did she do wrong? He pulls away slightly, revealing my face. He starts to wipe the hair out of my face. This feels nice. A man being nice to me, the warmth and security that the other sex can give is so, so, so, *oh crap, here I go again*, the sobbing starts.

"It's not just Auntie Janet, my husband left me for sweetcorn."

"I'm sorry he left you for who?" asks Frankie.

I then explain how we hadn't been getting on, how he seemed really pissed off with me recently and then the sweetcorn incident happened and pow, it's all over.

"Shit, and then on top of all that your Auntie Janet dies, oh, you poor thing." He grabs me again and pulls me into his bare chest. By the time I am released from Frankie's grasp, I realise I should have left about fifteen minutes ago to pick up Davina from school. Bollocks. I thank Frankie for his understanding, quickly gather my things and head out. I keep my head down as I pass reception. Steph is still there, her face is bright red. I see the back of Kitty's head, a shimmering blonde with very definite silver streaks. *Hah!* I can hear her: "And now I want to book for the month after that..."

By the time I reach the school, it is very obvious I am late. For a start, I am able to park the car right outside the school gates, which is a first. To avoid a ticket, I usually have to park at the village hall, which is a good ten minutes' walk to the school. I quickly check my face in the mirror to make sure it isn't obvious I have been crying. My eyes are puffy but the red blotches and snot have gone. I walk through the school gates; there are a few ways and strays, kids who have been kicking their football after school in the field and groups of parents who have clearly been chatting in the playground. As I reach the exit where Davina is usually delivered, I notice it's locked. I knock on the door. A cleaner is passing.

"We are closed."

How the fuck can you be closed, you are a school and it's only 15.55.

"My daughter is in there," I mouth back.

"You can't come in," she shouts.

What? Because I am late I am no longer able to retrieve my child? There would have been the odd occasion when I would have accepted this, especially after the time she threw her Baby Annabel at my head. An overnight stay at school might have done her some good. But not today, today I need my munchkin with me. I bang again.

"I want to get my daughter."

"You can't get her, you'll have to use the front door," she shouts back.

Well, why the fuck didn't she say that in the first place? I can see her tutting and pointing at me, telling another fellow cleaner.

I am let into the main school through the front doors by a lovely Scottish lady. I can't understand a word she says as she buzzes me through, but it's something about the main hall. At least I know where that is, thanks to the nativity. I walk into the giant hall. Mrs Crecher is at the front of the hall. Behind her are some small tables and chairs. The Crecher looks at me with narrow eyes. She does not utter a word but points to a table at the back. There are about six children, one of them being mine. Davina's head is face down. She doesn't see me as I walk up to her. When I am standing in front of her, I can see she is drawing a picture of what looks like her, Daddy and a stick lady with something coming out of her head, could that be flames?

"Davina," I say quietly. She sobs then she looks up at me. Her eyes fill with big fat tears.

"Mummy," she cries. "I didn't think you going to come." I scoop her up in my arms.

"I'm sorry darling, I got stuck in traffic and I'd left my phone at home."

"Silly mummy," she says, but clings onto me all the same.

I have to carry her to the car. I try to put her down but she clings on tighter. This is actually quite nice, I needed this too. When we get home, I promise to make her her favourite tea, spaghetti bolognaise. She settles in front of the telly with a large packet of chocolate buttons. She doesn't seem too damaged by what happened. The home phone rings.

"Daddy," I hear Davina say; she got to the phone before me. "Daddy, Mummy forgot to pick me up. I had to go in the main hall and do pictures. I did a picture for you, Daddy. Yes, I'll get mummy. See you Saturday."

She hands me the phone. I brace myself.

"Can I just say, I didn't forgot her, I got stuck in traffic."

"I didn't think you would forget her," he replies. Oh, I wasn't expecting that. "I'll pick her up Saturday at ten o'clock. We are going to my mother's and staying over. Can I drop her off after lunch on Sunday?"

"Yes, of course," I reply.

"Okay. Bye."

"Bye," I respond.

He puts the phone down. Ordinarily, I would have been really excited at the prospect of a child free weekend, but the very thought of it fills me with dread. What will I do with myself? I text Faye to see what she is up to but she and the kids are away at some relatives golden wedding anniversary in the Lakes. I think about Leigh but then remember she won't long have been back off honeymoon and I really cannot face a loved up, tanned Princess right now. Lou is off, apparently, on a charity overnight walk. She suggests I attend with her, but the thought of walking around the city, starting at midnight, finishing around eight a.m., with no alcohol really does not appeal to me. *So it's just me, then*, I think to myself. I decide I will go to the gym and perhaps a swim, then maybe fit in some shopping and watch a really trashy film on the telly, stuffing my face with crisps and Haribo and helping myself to copious amounts of Pinot Grigio. Sorted.

After Pete collects Davina, I make my way to the gym. Steph is on reception. Oh crap, will she be pissed off with me for disappearing yesterday?

"Jess," she calls me over. "Are you okay? Frankie told me about your Auntie Janet, you should have said something."

Crap, the lie has legs.

"I, er, you know, didn't want to make a fuss, I guess I was just feeling vulnerable and Kitty Vanderlosse was the straw that broke the camel's back. Thanks," I say, smiling at Steph. She smiles back. Well, at least I'm not in the shit, which is a relief.

I walk into the studio ready to set up my station for body pump. Jade bounces over to me. (I don't think she knows how to walk properly.) She places her hand on my arm.

"I'm so sorry to hear about your auntie, Jess," she says.

I nod. I daren't say another word for fear that I will be struck down by lightning from the gods above.

"Whenever anything bad happens to me, I find the best way is to stay active."

Of course you do, that's why there is not even a pimple that isn't toned on your perfect body.

"Thanks," I manage.

After pump, I decide to stay for Body Balance. Shame they don't have a Life Balance class. By the time I am finished I am beetroot red. I head downstairs to take a shower. As I get to the bottom of the steps, I bump into Frankie.

"Jess," he says. "How you feeling? I've been thinking about you." *You have?* "How you holding up?"

189

"I'm feeling much better today," I say. "Thanks for yesterday, it was good to just let it all out."

"Hey, that's what mates are for," he squeaks. "Listen, I'm on a break in ten, fancy a shake?"

A shake? I don't think I could face more exercise.

"Or a coffee if you prefer?" he asks.

Oh, a health shake.

"Yes, that would be, er, lovely."

"Great, I'll see you in ten." He heads back up the steps, taking about five at a time. I watch his muscular legs as he strides over the steps. He really is a fine specimen.

I have a quick shower, dry my hair and apply perhaps a little more make-up than needed. When I walk out in the drinks area, Frankie is already there. There are a few members of the PT staff with him.

"Hey, Jess, over here," he shouts. "Listen, a few of us are heading into town tonight if you fancy joining us?"

I look at the others to see if they approve of this invitation. Jason, Caroline, Maddy and Flynn are all looking at me with smiley, pity-filled eyes. Guess they too know about Auntie Janet. God help me if she ever joins this club, not that there is any chance of that.

"Come on, Jess, we are going into Leeds, a change of scenery will do you good," says Maddy. I don't think I have ever even spoken to Maddy before. I contemplate this a while, am I going to stay at home and watch Bridget Jones: The Edge of Reason and eat my entire body weight in crisps and Haribo, or should I actually just get a life and get out there? I decide on option two.

"Why not?" I say. The others disperse and I sit down with Frankie. The waitress walks over and hands me a protein shake.

"You should try this, it really helps rebuild your strength after exercise."

"Thanks," I say, looking at a large glass of muesli looking sludge.

Frankie and I aren't alone for long; he knows everyone in the gym. It is very clear he is some kind of god. The women fuss about him, the men respect him, sticking out their chests whenever they talk to him. The only one that doesn't seem that impressed is Keith the Tennis Coach.

"Hey, Keith, when you gonna let me build up those abs?"

"When you start spending your salary on food rather than supplements."

Ouch, that was a bit harsh. I'm sure Frankie eats a sensible, varied diet. Frankie doesn't seem bothered by Keith's comment. He lets it pass right over his head.

Frankie and I don't do much talking, very little actually. By the time everyone leaves us and Frankie has given advice to various members about which exercise they should try now, he tells me he has another PT session. We are meeting outside the gym tonight at seven p.m., when a mini bus will then take us into Leeds. *Whoop whoop.* I'm a little excited.

It takes me a good two hours to get ready. Everyone is much younger than me and although I am back to a reasonable size and more toned than I have ever been,

I'm not like them. I still have the odd lump and bulge I need to hide – having a baby does that to you. Earlier, after I had left the gym, I quickly called into the Designer Outlet and bought two dresses from Ted Baker. I couldn't decide which one but promised myself I would take which ever one I didn't wear back. My mum telephoned from the Costa Del Sol – she and my step-dad own an apartment out there.

"Well, I'm just glad you are getting back on the horse, love. There is no point moping about, if it's not right best you find out now rather than ten years later when you're fat and wrinkly and no-one wants you anymore." *Thanks, Mum.* "How you getting to Leeds?" she asks. "Don't be going in any taxi on your own, you know what those foreigners are like." This is interesting, coming from a woman who spends half the year surrounded by 'those foreigners'.

"There's a mini bus picking us up from the gym, I'm only getting a taxi to the gym, it's not that far."

"Why don't you see if Janet will give you a lift in? I've just spoken to her, she says her WI group have cancelled the meeting tonight, something to do with an outbreak of food poisoning. I'm not surprised, with all the bloody cake they eat."

Yes, that will go down well. Auntie Janet, back from the dead for one night only.

"Don't worry, mother. In fact, I have just had a text from Sarah, she wants to share a taxi in with me." I don't even know a Sarah. I'm getting good at this lying thing.

"Okay, love, well you be careful, I don't want any more grandchildren just yet." I make the necessary reassurances and hang up.

I'm ready. The taxi pulls into the driveway. I opted for the short black dress, which is tight but has enough ruffles down the front that it doesn't cling to my stomach. I've gone for the smokey eyes look and decide to wear those five inch heels I bought last summer that I've never dared leave the house in. *What the hell? It's time to try something new.* Thank goodness the streets of Leeds are paved, if they were cobbled or graveled like my driveway I would be in some serious ankle trouble. It took me a good five minutes to walk down the drive to the taxi. I'm sure it was a source of amusement for the taxi driver.

Everyone is there when I get to the gym. Frankie looks seriously hot. He is wearing tight black trousers and a silk based shirt, open to below his pectorals, obviously. Steph and Jade are also there, which is a relief – particularly Steph, anyway. Leah is still unwell so couldn't make it, which is a huge relief. I couldn't cope with forty minutes of her endless chatter. I sit next to Steph on the coach. Despite being my manager, she is a year younger than me and is actually a really nice girl. Maddy hands everyone a small shot glass on the bus and pours in neat vodka. I hate the bloody stuff but, to avoid being a bad sport, I knock it back. By the time we reach Leeds, a few of them are clearly well on their way to being inebriated. Maddy and Caroline are singing Lady Marmalade, I'm surprised they even know the song, they must only be about twelve.

We get dropped off outside the Corn Exchange and are being picked up at one o'clock. Jeez, I'm not sure I can last that long with this lot. We move from bar to bar. I can't seem to find my drink. No-one wants prosecco and I can't neck wine. The way we are moving through the bars, I'll only have had a couple of sips. I decide to go for a Bacardi and coke. It was one of my younger days' drinks. I check to see what Frankie is drinking; he's not drinking beer or lager, I guess there are too many calories in there. I walk over to him to ask.

"What's that?" I ask.

"It's a mixture of orange, tomato juice and Worcester sauce with a splash of brandy. Here, try some."

It looks bloody revolting. I give it a taste. *Yuck.*

"Not my thing," I say, handing it back.

"I limit myself to four of these on a night out. I never get a hangover. It gives me the energy I need the following morning to do a 10K run." *Wow. To be that controlled.* If only I had that off switch, I'd be financially so much better off. "Do you like it in here?" he asks. I look around. It's just an ordinary bar, there is nothing particularly special about it, it's filled with the usual towny types. I notice Frankie is getting a lot of attention from the opposite and quite a lot from the same sex too.

"It's okay," I say. I'm not really sure what else to say.

"I hate places like this," he says.

"So why did you come?" I ask, slightly perplexed.

"Because I thought you needed a night out." *Oh, how sweet.* I feel a little coy, I want to play with my hair and the hem of my skirt.

"That's really kind of you, but you didn't need to. I'll be fine, honestly."

"I also thought it would be a good way to get to know you better." *Aye up. Frankie the Gym God wants to get to know me better? Just how much better? Don't get carried away,* I tell myself. He may just want to suggest additional exercises to tighten various parts of my body.

"Shall we go sit down?" he asks. I nod. He leads me to a table with two chairs right in the back of the corner. It is difficult to hear him because the music is so loud – the fact he has a slightly squeaky voice doesn't help either. He's not saying much, I guess making conversation isn't his strong point.

"How did you get to becoming a PT?" I ask. Clearly this is a topic he likes to discuss. He takes me through his childhood, how he was the fat kid at school and bullied. It's the usual story of fat boy turns into a teenager, sheds the weight and starts training. He was brought up by his grandmother as his mother was an alcoholic and he never knew his father. His mother died just when he started sitting his G.C.S.Es, which hit him hard and is the only reason why he didn't pass any of them. He was working out all the time at the local gym and started helping to clear up. He worked his way up through the gym and is now exceptionally proud to be the head PT trainer at Charles Frogman. After he finally finishes his life story, I realise that my story isn't perhaps quite as bad. Yes, my marriage has failed, but I had a good upbringing. I too didn't know my real father – my mother always told me

195

it was one of three possibilities – but I have a great step-dad.

A few of the others have left already. Flynn and Steph walk over and ask if we are ready to head off. Frankie looks at me. I'm really not that fussed about going anywhere else. I like it here. Flynn and Steph decide they will join us. It's not quite what I envisaged, but at least it's just us four.

We spend the next several hours laughing. Frankie is actually easier to talk to when there are others around. It's not because he likes to show off, I think he is just actually quite shy and responds better to groups. Before I know it, it's 12.50, the mini bus is picking us up in ten minutes. I need the toilet. As I stand up to leave, Frankie stands too. "Where are you going, Jess?"

"I'm just off to the ladies," I reply, slightly pleased he is interested in where I am going.

"Here, let me help you," he asks.

Help me? Help me to what, have a piss? He can see the question on my face.

"The toilets are downstairs, I don't think you should be walking down there on your own with those heels." *Oh, right. How sweet.* He's so protective. A true gent. I grab his arm and he escorts me down to the ladies toilet. Thankfully, there isn't a large queue as most people have moved on. He waits outside until I am done and then escorts me back up the stairs.

"You are a true gent," I tell him.

"It's my pleasure, I'm used to doing it for my grandmother."

Erm, I don't think that's meant quite how it sounds, I tell myself.

"Jess," he says, stopping me before we get back into the bar. "I really like spending time with you, I thought that maybe I could cook you dinner one night next week perhaps?"

I'm taken aback. The Gym God now wants to cook me dinner.

"I'd love that."

"Great."

Then he leans in and kisses me. It's a soft kiss. He feels really warm. Just as I am getting into it, he withdraws, takes my hand and walks me back to the Flynn and Steph. On the way back, Frankie and I sit at the back of bus holding hands. It's sweet, I mean, romantic. He sees me safely into the taxi I pre-booked to pick me up from the gym. When I get home, I feel light-headed and happy. I walk into the kitchen and see the answer phone flashing. There are five new messages.

"Jess, it's me, please pick up. Something's happened. We are on our way to the hospital. It's Davina. I'll try your mobile."

Crap, I didn't take my mobile out. I press for the next message.

"Your mobile isn't answering. We are at York Hospital. Call me. Pete."

I don't listen to the rest. I'm shaking. I dial Pete's number. He answers.

"Oh Jess, thank God you've called…"

Chapter Fifteen
My Worst Nightmare

I'm in the taxi on my way to the hospital. Thankfully, our local taxi firm, Top Cars, are very loyal and sent the same car straight back. The journey in seems to be taking forever. There are no cars on the road since it's the very early hours. *Why is it taking so long?* All kind of horrid thoughts are running through my head.

I've never heard Pete sound so scared. It turns out Davina had had a meltdown at his parents' house. He had put her to bed but she had kicked off because she wanted me. He had shouted at her and shut the bedroom door. Without him realising, she had run out of the house into his parent's woodland. When he realised she was missing, he ran outside and found her climbing up a tree. The branch broke and she fell to the ground and was knocked unconscious. The ambulance staff couldn't rouse her. He had been ringing me. They were now in the intensive care unit. She had a suspected subdural hematoma (brain bleed). They had managed to stabilise her at the hospital but she wasn't talking. When I spoke to Pete, they were waiting for her to be taken for a CT scan.

When I finally reach the hospital, one of the night porters directs me to the intensive care unit. It's amazing how quickly and easily you can walk in five inch heels when you need to. When I arrive in intensive care, the first people I see are Pete's parents, who are sat in the lounge waiting area.

"Oh, Jessica!" cries Pete's mother. She looks a mess.

"Where are they?" I ask. I haven't time for pleasantries.

"We are waiting for them to get back from the scan."

I head to the nursing station so I can be taken to my daughter. The matron looks up. She looks me up and down and like a penny suddenly drops, she says, "Ah, you must be Davina's mum."

"Where are they?" I ask. I haven't time for judgement right now, I need to see my daughter.

"They are on their way back from Radiography. They will be here any minute. You can wait in there."

She directs me to a room directly opposite the nursing station. Within seconds, I hear a trolley and Davina is wheeled in by the porters. With her is a nurse. Behind is a clearly traumatised Pete. I reach straight for Davina. Oh god, my baby, my poor baby. She looks so small on this bed, she looks so out of place. She doesn't belong here. I feel like I'm in some kind of nightmare. There is dried blood on her face from the scratches.

"Oh, Pete." I throw myself into his arms. "What did they say, what's wrong with her?"

The nurse interrupts. "The doctor will be here shortly, love. He's checking the scan and just waiting on some other tests before he comes to see you. Can I get you anything? A tea, coffee?" I shake my head. I can barely breathe.

Pete and I sit either side of Davina. I keep stroking her hair. Pete's head is in his hands. I'm half expecting him to ask where I have been. I feel so guilty for being out and not being at home for her. If I'd have stayed at home, I would have been straight there, been with her during the scan... I sob.

"It's all my fault, Jess," says Pete. "I snapped at her. I told her she couldn't go home. She begged me to let her go home but I wouldn't let her."

"It isn't your fault at all, you didn't do anything wrong." I can see he doesn't believe me. He will never forgive himself. The door opens, we both stand. It's Pete's mother.

"I've brought you a coffee each and a sandwich. You need to keep up your strength." Bless her, I know she's trying to help, but I really can't face eating or drinking anything. She turns to me. "Jess, I'm so sorry, she was in our care, I told John he needed to cut that tree down, the branches are too low, I..."

"Not now, mother," snaps Pete. Carol looks hurt. She loiters for a while, then John arrives.

"Come on, Carol, let's give them some space. You'll text us, won't you, when you hear something? I think we'll go for a walk." John escorts a reluctant Carol out of the room.

Within a couple of seconds, the door opens again, "Oh for fuck's sake, mother..." But's it's the doctor this time. He pulls up a chair and has the scan picture in his hands. He holds up the scan and points to a shaded area.

"So, as you can see, there has been small bleed in the brain." *Oh God.* My hand is over my mouth. I'm transfixed on the doctor, listening to his every word. "Fortunately, the bleeding has stopped." Relief. *This is good, right?*

"So she's going to be okay?" I plead.

"It's difficult to say for certain at this stage what impact the bleed will have on her, there can be a loss of memory sometimes and her speech may be affected." I can't breathe again. "However, she is stable, her vitals are good and she is out of immediate danger." And breathe again.

"So what does this mean?" asks Pete.

"It means we need to keep her under observation for the next few days to see how she responds generally. If all is well…"

"She can come home?" I ask.

"If all is well, then, certainly, there is a good chance she can come home." It's not quite the answer I was hoping for, but I'll take it. The doctor leaves and tells us he will be back again later in the morning. The nurse comes back in.

"Shall I bring in a camp bed?" she asks. Pete nods. "I'm afraid we only have one, the others are being used."

"It's okay," he says. "Jess can have it."

We both spend the next few hours in silence, listening to every breath out of Davina's mouth, watching her as she moves. At one point, she lets out a little cry; she must be dreaming, but still, I ring for the nurse to check she is okay. The nurse checks the ping machine, she is fine. At some time around seven, I wake up to a small cry. I must have dropped off. For a split second, I am clueless as to where I am, but then I remember. Davina is stirring. She is groaning.

"Sweetheart, sweetheart, it's Mummy." Her eyes are starting to open.

"Mummy," she sobs. Pete has buzzed for the nurse.

"It's okay, darling, we are here."

"Where am I?"

"You are in the hospital, darling. You had a fall." Pete can't speak, he's ashen faced.

"Where's Mr Ted Ted?" she asks. I look at Pete. I can see more panic on his face.

"It's at my mother's," he mouths.

"Mr Ted Ted is having a lovely sleepy morning at Gan Gan's house."

"I want Mr Ted Ted," she sobs. The nurse is in the room. She checks the machine, checks her pulse, checks the IV drip.

"Good morning, sweetheart. Aren't you a pretty thing?" the nurse says to Davina. Davina scowls a little. She doesn't like people being too familiar with her. "I'll call for the doctor," says the nurse.

"Why?" I ask, panic-stricken.

"Don't worry, love, I said I would beep him when she wakes up."

"Text your parents, Pete, to let them know she is awake." Pete grabs his phone. He looks so lost. Men really aren't that great in a crisis.

"What shall I say?" he asks.

"Just tell them she's awake and the doctor is coming, we will let them know more when we know more." Pete taps away. Within a couple of minutes, Carol pokes her head through the door.

"Morning, Princess," she says. Davina doesn't respond. She stares at Gan Gan, pretending to be sheepish. Carol looks dreadful. I've never seen her without make-up. Bless them, they must have spent the night in the family lounge.

"Listen," I say, "you guys need to go and get cleaned up, we will text you once the doctor has been. Go get some rest and come back later." Carol doesn't look convinced, but Pete is nodding.

"Mother, please, just do as Jess asks. We will keep you informed." Reluctantly, Carol leaves the room.

The doctor arrives a short time later. He goes through a series of tests with Davina, most of which she is unwilling to participate in. She moves her legs and arms willingly, but when asked to say her name and her age, she point blank refuses.

"Come on, darling, just do as the doctor asks."

"No," she replies. The doctor smiles. I feel like I should apologise.

"Don't worry, Miss Davina, you get some rest. Dr Roberts will come and see you again later."

"Can I have a word, please?" asks the doctor. *Oh crap, are we going to get bollocked because our daughter won't do as she is told?*

"She seems fine to me."

"But she wouldn't answer," I say.

"Yes, but she knew the question. I'm not concerned. It seems to me she's not not talking because she can't, she's not talking because she doesn't want to. I'm off duty now until tomorrow, Dr Roberts will be taking over and she will be along later to see how she is doing. Don't worry." He puts his hand on my shoulder. "She's out the woods." He laughs at his little joke.

"Pete, I need some stuff from home, do you think your parents will pick up some stuff for me?"

"I'll do it," says Pete. I think he's relieved to have a job. I give him a list of things I need for Davina and me. He kisses Davina on the head and reassures her he will be back soon and promises to bring Mr Ted Ted with him, and Mrs Bun Bun. He then kisses me on top of the head. I put on the television for Davina and she watches her favourite show, Mr Tumble, and falls asleep half way through Woolly and Tig. I'm now in the mood for coffee. I leave the room and tell the staff at the nurses station that I'm just going into the kitchen to make coffee and that I'll be straight back. They give me a reassuring nod and a "Don't worry, dear, we will keep an eye on her." There are quite a few other people in the kitchen, helping themselves to coffee and toast. No-one seems to notice or be particularly bothered by me in my short black dress and five inch heels. As I pour the hot water onto my coffee, I suddenly have the overwhelming need to throw up. *Oh crap, can I make it out of here in time to the toilet?* As I head out of the kitchen, my five inch heels are once again a problem. I stumble, then comes the splatter as my vomit hits the cold stark floor of the hospital wing. Oh fuck. Thankfully, being in a hospital, no-one really reacts that much to seeing vomit. One of the health assistants comes over with a mop and bucket. It seems as though she was on standby, waiting for this to happen. I begin to wonder if people think it's because I was out getting shit faced last night whilst my daughter was being brought to hospital. Whilst it wouldn't necessary be wrong for them to think that is what happened, the truth is I wasn't drunk last night. I struggled to find my drink – after two Bacardi and cokes, I couldn't face another alcoholic drink. I just fancied lime and soda water – so much so, I must have had about eight. You can't be sick from too many limes and soda, can you? A kind nurse comes up to me.

"Shall I get you a gown to wear, love?"

"Yes please," I say, feeling embarrassed and emotional.

"Follow me, pet."

I follow her into one of the storage rooms. She hands me a gown. I take it and burst into tears. She hugs me, a proper mother type hug. She doesn't care that I stink of vomit and God knows what else, she just lets me sob on her shoulder and keeps saying, "There, there." She leaves me to get changed, which I do as quickly as possible. I need to get back to Davina. I stuff my outfit into the bin, I won't be needing that again. I head out of the room and back to Davina's room, wearing a hospital gown and dressing gown with five inch heels. It's an interesting look.

Pete arrives back a little later with two holdalls. One for me and one for Davina. He looks a little quizzical at my attire but chooses not to ask. Since he's back, I need to get freshened up. He stays with Davina whilst I go and shower. I take the holdall into the bathroom. He's put the clothes in I asked for, my Abercrombie jogging bottoms and jumper, a pair of jeans and a couple of loose fitting tops. However, instead of pyjamas, he's put in my silk over the knee nightie. *WTF?* I check for some underwear: there is not a single pair of cotton pants in there. I have five pairs of lace trimmed G-string pants, most of which cut into me still. They are the select few I kept because they are from Agent Provocateur and I could never bring myself to throw them out. Oh well, at least he tried.

After a shower and freshen up, I am feeling a bit better. When I go back into the room, Pete and Davina are sat playing snap. "Snap," shouts my little lamb. It wasn't a snap but I can tell Pete isn't going to question it. He is now forever hers, from here on in anything she wants is hers. If she wants a golden egg then by jove will she have a golden egg, even if he has to lay it himself. I settle in the chair and watch the two of them. It feels like old times, the good old times. Pete looks across and smiles. I can tell he feels it too.

Dr Roberts visits us later and tells us she is really happy with Davina's progress. The latest CT scan raised no concerns and she thinks that, in another couple of days, she will be able to go home. We are moved from Intensive Care onto the children's ward, which is a slight shame only for the fact that we are now on a ward as opposed to having our own room. Only one parent is allowed to stay over so Pete and I agree I will stay. Carol and John arrive later. Carol turns up on the ward, dressed and groomed like the Carol I know; there is not a hair out of place. She is carrying a large picnic hamper. Inside there are cold turkey sandwiches, cordial, spring water, fruit, nuts, cake, the works. I thank her, recognising that this is what she need to do to make herself feel useful, and I am grateful. I've always hated canteen food so a homemade picnic hamper suits me a great deal and I am beginning to feel famished. Carol and John stay for about an hour then leave us. Pete helps me bathe Davina and get her into her night gear. After she is tucked up in bed with Mr Ted Ted and Mrs Bun Bun, he kisses her forehead and promises her he will be back tomorrow. Again, as Pete leaves he kisses me, on the cheek this time. I'd forgotten how I loved Pete's lips. I've missed the feel of them.

I had a crappy night's sleep listening to everyone else's child fart, sneeze, and cry. Although the worst had to be listening to the ten year old in the cubicle next door to ours having a shit. He was clearly constipated. "Come on, Thomas, you can do it, just squeeze it out," said his mother. After several minutes of grunting and saying, "I can't, I can't," he clearly could, as the smell of shit was forever evident. Twit and Twat were born that night – well, that's the name I gave to the two large plops I heard into the bed pan. Davina, bless her, slept through the whole night. When she woke the next morning, she clearly had had a great night's sleep. She looked rested and had some colour back in her cheeks. I wouldn't have cared if I didn't sleep at all, to see her starting to look like her old self is priceless. Whilst Davina went to sit with the other children to have some breakfast, I decided to go and get some coffee. I stepped into the kitchen area where fresh coffee was being brewed. The smell hit me at once. Oh fuck, not again. I made a run for it. This time I made it to the toilets in time. Five minutes later I emerge from the bathroom. Just as I was walking out the door, the same nurse who had helped me yesterday was there. "Not well again?" she asked quizzically. This time there was no suggestion I'd been out on a bender, she mainly worked on the children's ward and had seen me here last night.

"Yes, I think it must be the worry and tiredness from the past couple of days. I'm sure it's all fine."

"People aren't generally sick two days in a row, particularly in a morning, love." *Aren't they?* She eyes me suspiciously. Perhaps I'm like E.T. and have absorbed some of Davina's feelings? "Tell you what, love, since you are in here anyway, just to be on the safe side, pee into this for me, will you?" *Ah, of course, cross contamination.* If it's a sickness bug, I can't stay on the ward. I do as she asks and give her a sample. I never knew wee would tell you if you have a sickness bug, but then medicine and technology has changed so much over the years. However, my biggest fear is I do have a bug and firstly, I've infected the children's ward and secondly, I can't stay with Davina, which would break both our hearts. *No, it won't be a bug*, I reassure myself. *I bet it's just tiredness, everyone is different.*

Pete arrives later that morning. I go outside to check my phone. I'd texted Steph on the Sunday to say I wouldn't be in work this week, explaining in brief about Davina. I had several voice messages on my phone, one from my mother, after talking her out of getting on plane back here, I promised her I would keep her up to date. I will ring her next. One is from Faye, sending her best, the other is from Auntie Janet and finally, the last one is from Frankie. He sounds extra squeaky on voicemail. "Hi Jess, it's Frankie. Steph told me about Davina. I hope she is okay. I miss you. Call me when you can." I'm struck with a pang of guilt. Not towards Frankie but towards Pete. I can't think about it right now. I walk back into the hospital. When I enter the ward, the kind nurse asks for a quick word. She can see the panic on my face. "Davina is fine, love, she's colouring with her dad." She takes me into the quiet room. "So, I tested your sample and it's as I suspected…" *Oh no, a bloody sickness bug.* "Did you know you are pregnant?" *What the, how the, when the…*my face must say it all. "I take it that no, you didn't." She sits me down on the couch. "It's a bit of a shock, I guess, but a lovely shock. Your husband will be delighted, he was telling me yesterday how he wanted more kids." *Pete, it can't be Pete's.* We haven't had sex since London and that was about twelve weeks ago. But there hasn't been anyone else, I kissed Frankie but that doesn't make babies. The nurse can see my mind is whirling. "I'll give you a minute, the test suggests you are about seven weeks," she says. She leaves the room.

I'm thinking. I try to remember all the things I've done, then it hits me: the wedding, Leigh and Jason's wedding. I got really pissed. I couldn't remember anything the next morning, I woke up naked but there is nothing new there; after I've been drinking, sometimes I go to sleep fully clothed, other times, I strip. We must have had sex. But didn't I have a period? No. I haven't had a period. I suddenly remember thinking about this the other week but I wasn't worried because I knew I hadn't had sex with anyone and just put it down to all the upset and stress. When the nurse returns, I appear a little pleased.

"Don't worry," I say, "I've worked it out. The wedding, it must have been at the wedding."

"Right, dear, well, congratulations."

Yeah I know, phew, I've worked it out. Well done, me. And then it hits me, pregnant, baby, *I'm pregnant, holy shit, I'm going to have a baby.* Once again, my lack of poker face says it all.

"Children are a blessed thing, pet, they are gifts and are given to us for a reason. You should cherish them, enjoy them – they don't stay children forever. One day they grow up. Enjoy them whilst you can, love." After that profound statement, she leaves. *Think Jess, think*, I tell myself. What to do. I decide I'm not going to tell Pete yet. We have too much else to worry about for now. In fact, I'm going to put it to the back of my mind until we get home.

The next day, Davina is allowed to come home. Thank the heavens. I am genuinely relieved, not just because she has been given the all clear but also because I will no longer be woken by the smell of Thomas's shit. Pete brings us back home. It's later in the day by the time we reach home, as there is no such thing as a quick check out from hospital. Not just because we are delivering chocolates and thank you cards to all the wonderful staff but just the number of checks on Davina that need to be undertaken before she can leave. I am not grumbling. I wouldn't have it any other way.

Pete stays to share a frozen pizza and chips with us. There isn't really much else in. He stays until Davina is in bed. After she is safely tucked up in bed, a sight which I have been praying for these past few days, I head back downstairs to Pete. He is stood in the kitchen.

"Right well, I guess I will head off." It's written all over his face. I can tell he doesn't want to go. I don't want him to go.

"I'm pregnant," I announce. My mouth decided not to engage with my brain first, clearly. He looks at me.

"Who's the father?"

"You are, you great dope," I respond, a little harsh perhaps.

"But, but…"

"I'm seven weeks. I've worked it out. Leigh and Jason's wedding, remember?" He still doesn't look sure.

211

"Pete, I haven't been with anyone else. It has to be the wedding."

"But I thought, when I saw you at the hospital the night Davina was taken in," he winces, "I assumed you were out with someone else, that you had someone else."

"I was on a work night out, Pete, there hasn't been and isn't anyone else." Another small lie, but it's half true, anyway. He looks to his feet then back to me; his eyes are glistening. "Pete, we are having a child and I want…" I'm putting myself out on a line here, "… I want to have this child with you, to be a family again." He is staring now. *Oh shit, what if he says no, get stuffed?* I really hadn't thought this through, I should have thought out a better plan to tell him, one perhaps where he felt compelled to stay with me.

"That's all I want, Jess. I want to be with you and Davina and the baby."

He walks over and places his hand on my belly. We hug and cry and hug and cry. The music in my ears has burst into a crescendo of string music and so now we will live happily ever after…

Chapter Sixteen
The Next Chapter

Bailey came into this world screaming. Another C-section, and he certainly didn't want to be disturbed from his comfy surroundings. I cannot deny I was relieved when he came out, not because I didn't enjoy being fat and having swollen ankles and constantly needing to urinate – in fact, I quite like all that side of it – it was more the concern that he might come out looking like a bottle of Pinot Grigio. I had had a very frank discussion with my GP about the amount of alcohol I had consumed in those early weeks. My GP was not particularly sympathetic, which I totally get, but when I first saw Bailey, I could tell he was perfect.

It's easier with the second child. You know what to expect this time. Your life has already been turned upside down so another addition really doesn't matter. There are, of course, the worries of how Davina will be: will she be jealous, will she hurt him, but the nice thing about having a child slightly older, she knows she cannot colour on his head (after I told her, anyway). Those first twelve weeks which I prayed, counted down each millisecond, with Davina, go by in a breeze with your second. In fact, I want to stop time. I want him to stay as my gorgeous bundle, my last child (definitely last, Pete has had the snip). I think there is also something about boys, they are much easier going. I think if I'd have had Bailey first, Davina might have come along much quicker. I prefer it this way round though, imagine how horrid it would be to have your first child easy going and then the second be hell on legs. It's happened to close friends of mine. They are the friends who are on first names terms with the salesman from the Virgin Wine Club.

Another difference I have noted between the first and the second child – the second will actually sit in front of the television and watch CBeebies from about seven weeks old, Davina wasn't interested until aged three. Also, Bailey actually eats and appears to enjoy my home made blended gourmet meal, i.e. the bottom of the veg drawer from the fridge all cooked and mushed together. He's actually appreciative. When I gave Davina my homemade food, she chose to blow raspberries so it went all over the travertine flooring. If I ever gave Davina baby jars she would look at me like I'd just forced her to eat her own nappies (to be fair, they do look similar to how they come out). I'm starting to feel like one of those organic cake-making bitches since Bailey eats everything I make for him.

The biggest difference, though, is how complete I feel. That's not to say I don't love my daughter because I do, I adore her, most days anyway. However, there is something that happened to me when I had Bailey, maybe it's because I never felt good enough as a parent the first time around and this time I am getting it right, or maybe it's being a family of four that suits us better. I like the fact we had a boy. I always felt responsible for Davina in every department. When it comes to female issues, over to me, clothing issues, over to me, it's as though she is entirely my responsibility because she is a girl. However, add a boy to the mix and it's Pete's turn, not the clothing, obviously – poor thing would permanently be dressed up looking like an Ewok. I can honestly say, though, the void has been filled.

As for Pete and I, we are back on track. He is sulking a little because I made him have a vasectomy and his balls swelled to the size of footballs, but it was only a couple of days of pain. He still grumbles that I make him wear a condom when we have sex. I don't like the mess. I never told him about Frankie. There was nothing in it, really. Of course, when I told Frankie that Pete and I were getting back together, he was most upset. I swear I saw a tear. I did feel bad, another woman letting him down. The reality is, it would have never worked. If I closed my eyes to listen to him whisper sweet nothings, it would have been like I was dating Alvin from the Chipmunks. Frankie is more of a visual person, for me, anyway. Within a few weeks, he smiled at me again. He and Steph seemed to be getting on rather well. He was showing her how to squat. The sight of that is enough to make me never eat a cheese burger again. I'm just a member again at the gym now. I quit my reception job when I fell pregnant. I always feared that with my raging pregnancy hormones I would actually grab Kitty Vanderlosse's tennis racket and ram it up her arse.

It's coming up to our ten year wedding anniversary. Pete has a surprise for me. His parents are coming to stay and we are having a two night mini break. I'm really excited, although a little apprehensive – it's the first time just Pete and I have been away together since London. However, things are different now. Once Pete and I got back together, he told me that he had just forgotten how to have fun. He turned forty and went into some kind of mid-life crisis. Instead of buying a Porsche and shagging a twenty year old, he became serious, felt he needed to focus on his career to make sure he earned enough for our retirement. He forgot how to let go and relax. He now says he doesn't care if I try flag down a bus after his works Christmas party, or if my boob pops out my dress when we are at a wedding, when I am on the stage, trying to sing with the band and my strap pops. That's just me, it's who I am, and he loves me for it. Like I always say, you knew what you signed up for.

It's really difficult knowing what to pack for a mystery weekend away. I assume it's this country, so I will need waterproofs and something warm, but will we be going out for meals? Yes, of course we will. I throw in the other dress I bought from Ted Baker when we were separated. I can now fit in it again. After kissing the kids goodbye and promising Davina to buy her a surprise, we head off in the car. I keep trying to get clues from Pete, but he's not giving anything anyway. It's 4.30 p.m. on a Friday, we can't be driving far at this time of night. Quicker than I expected, after just thirty minutes in the car we turn off the M18 and head for Doncaster.

Seriously? Doncaster? Is that the best you can do, Pete? Perhaps there is a luxury hotel there with fantastic spa, or maybe a castle for a murder mystery evening. Pete is following the signs for Doncaster airport. Hold the phone.

"Airport? Are we going to the airport, Pete?"

"Might be," he replies, which obviously means yes.

Holy cow, this is exciting. I hate spas anyway. Too many people making too much fuss over you. Crap, what if it's hot, I didn't pack a bikini. Oh well, I can buy one at the airport.

"Will it be hot?"

He smiles.

"Have I been there before?"

Nothing back.

"Is it a long flight?"

Still nothing.

"An hour, two?"

"For fuck's sake, Jess, just wait, will you?"

We pull into the car park at the airport and get a short stay ticket. As we enter the airport he stops me.

"Right, now I'll tell you, because you are going to find out soon. Prague, we are off to Prague. You said how beautiful and romantic it was, so I thought we'd go together."

"Oh," I say, a little surprised. Prague was the last place I'd have expected.

"Are you not happy?"

"Of course I am, I'm just surprised that's all."

"Well, here's the bigger surprise: we are staying at the Four Seasons. Arman agreed a reduced rate."

HOLY SHIT!